T0381236

A Captivating Mélange of People, Places & Mystical Coincidences

# TAWAFUQ
## WHATEVER WILL BE WILL BE

Sabiha Imran

# TAWAFUQ

## WHATEVER WILL BE WILL BE

This is not a book of fiction. All events and people as described are real. While some names have been changed to protect privacy. Others are mentioned after getting permission

Permissions
"Quotation of Albert Einstein in chapter 'The Big Move', page 177 is reproduced from George Sylvester Viereck's Glimpses of the Great (London: Duckworth, 1930), p. 376, with thanks and permission from the Estate of George Viereck."
The picture of the student(s), and the then Principal in the courtyard of St. Joseph School Karachi in the chapter 'The Early Years'; page 46 is reproduced with permission by The Citizens Archive of Pakistan

iUniverse books may be ordered through booksellers or by contacting:

iUniverse
1663 Liberty Drive
Bloomington, IN 47403, USA
www.iuniverse.com
1-800-Authors (1-800-288-4677)

Cover Concept & Design by Sabiha Imran

ISBN: 978-1-5320-8323-5 (hc)
ISBN: 978-1-5320-7374-8 (sc)
ISBN: 978-1-5320-7375-5 (e)

Library of Congress Control Number: 2019909027

Print information available on the last page.

iUniverse rev. date: 10/23/2019

# *Messages*

**Message from Gen. (Rted).  Pervez Musharraf,**
**Ex President of Pakistan**

President Pervez Musharraf
March 8, 2019

Sabiha Imran is a well known family friend. Her zest for life has manifested itself through a love of nature and a pursuit of various forms of artistic expression. Sabiha specializes in calligraphic art in which she has acquired recognition. Besides her immersion in various forms of art, her observation of personalities and situations has been so profound that she has molded her life based on them. These are equally meaningful for others. I have personally learnt a lot about her own family through her writing.

I wish her success in all future endeavors.

**General (Retd). Pervez Musharraf**
**Former President and Ex Chief of Staff, Pakistan Army**

## Message from Syed Babar Ali

I know Sabiha and her husband, Hafeez Imran, with whom I have been associated for the last forty years. I have witnessed her growth over the years, spiritually and as a person.

Sabiha is a great artist and I have seen her work, which I find most admirable. I did not realize that she writes as well as she paints.

Her book is a good read. It tells her story and the influence on her life's journey through her interaction with some extraordinary people. The striking thing for me is her perceptive mind, which keeps on absorbing the good she finds among the many people who have had an influence on her personality. As all artists are, she is very observant and has a tremendous learning attitude.

I consistently saw a thread of compassion, generosity and spirituality weaved throughout the book seamlessly in a way that truly manifests how one's experiences through life can shape one's perspectives.

This is her first book, but she has managed to pen her thoughts in a clear, engaging manner, which holds the reader's attention right till the end. The reader will feel as they were with her, sharing those memorable moments.

I wish her all the best in her endeavors.

**Syed Babar Ali, OBE**
**Entrepreneur, Educationist, and Ex Finance Minister of Pakistan**

## Message from Prof. Deep Saini

I first discovered Sabiha Imran's talent at an exhibition of her paintings in Mississauga in 2012. I was taken by how accessible her art really was – speaking beautifully through a rich variety of media, laying transparent her innermost feelings and values, for all to enjoy, without unduly straining the imagination. In *Tawafuq,* she has harnessed that same innate gift to paint with beautiful words a picture of her life's experiences that is just as much joy to read as her paintings are to behold.

Sabiha's style is inviting, drawing the reader with the informality of her 'girl next door' style, to travel alongside her through the journey of her life, intimately participating in her myriad experiences from her youth in the emergent Pakistan of the 1950s and 60s through an exciting global journey to today. *Tawafuq* — 'Whatever Will be, Will be' — is just that, a spontaneous immersion into an intimate experience of the 'open book' that is Sabiha.

**Deep Saini**
**Vice-Chancellor & President**
**University of Canberra**
**Australia**

## Message from Sultan Ghalib al-Qu'aiti

I was pleasantly surprised when Sabiha Imran, a family friend of long-standing, forwarded to me the pre-published manuscript of her first foray into the field of literature, bearing the mystifying title, "Tawafuq", meaning "Coincidence" or "Conformity" in Arabic, Persian and Turkish, as well as in Urdu; even though the text was in English! It did not take me long to realize that though a gifted artist, who till now has been expressing her thoughts and feelings on the canvas, she has now decided to attempt to do so in words as well.

"Tawafuq" is a reflection into aspects of her life's journey which has spanned continents, with focus on a number of pleasant, but unusual and unexpected experiences. These often involved people from diverse and unlikely backgrounds whom she stresses have helped her to learn, shape and develop better what she considers to be the true essence of compassion, kindness and spirituality. In short, anything that was to leave an indelible imprint on her heart, mind and person and influence her perspective on life. These encounters she reckons not to have been without a Divine purpose and meaning.

A feature of the book is that the author, treating it at times in the manner of a novel, does not burden her prospective readership with too many names and details. This I suppose introduces an element of surprise and anticipation. Her experiences and happenings presented by her as a string of cameos in a language and descriptive style uniquely her own; straight from the heart, with the genuine passion and enthusiasm expected of a true emotional artist when feeling inspired or excited about her subject. A common theme that appears to emerge and captures the essence of all these personal tales is the portrayal of the equality of all men before the Almighty and Eternal Creator. She dwells on the fact that how close they really are to each other, despite all the distinguishing features imposed by geographical and environmental, as well as ethnic factors.

"Tawafuq" is not just about "Coincidences" but a depiction of a series of encounters and events that were destined, according to the author to come together to shape and color her life. These she now wishes to share with others by this exercise and convey the innate wisdom of those whom she considers to have influenced her so deeply.

May this journey of hers be long, prosperously and fruitful for her and her family.

**Sultan Ghalib al-Qu'aiti -**
**Former Sultan of the Qu'aiti State in Hadhramaut**
**M.A. (Hons.) Oxon, M.A. (Hons.) Cantab**

# Contents

# Dedication

This book is dedicated to:

My parents- Fayyazi and Mahmud Minhas; whose love, wisdom and dedication, can never be acknowledged enough, also to my brothers, Haroon, Farooq, and Arif.

My sons -- Samir, Asim and Omar who are a blessing and the joys of my life,

My lovely daughter in laws- Zareen, Sana, Gulrukh and my grandchildren, Bilal, Zayd, Amal, Zaydan and Amani.

My husband Hafeez Imran; without whom this journey would have been incomplete.

# Acknowledgements

I would like to thank and express my gratitude to a few very special people who made this book possible by their encouragement and valuable suggestions and for their kind words and messages on completion and for being a part of my personal journey.

### General (Retd) Pervez Musharraf; Former President of Pakistan

It is certainly very rare for somebody to combine so many qualities in his person - leadership, humility, courage, and compassion. General Pervez Musharraf (Retd.) is one of this rare breed. He rose to the highest ranks; both in his chosen career as a professional soldier and then as the President of a country.

I personally experienced his larger than life personality on meeting him. He so graciously and kindly went out of his way to pen a few words about my book; words which means so much to me and which I will cherish and treasure. My heartfelt thanks and wishes for his prosperous, long healthy life.

### Sultan Ghalib al Qu'aiti; Former Sultan of the Qu'aiti State in Hadhramaut

Sincere thanks to Sultan Ghalib al-Qu'aiti, a well-respected family friend, possessing distinct old world charm, with a passion for history and a love for humanity in general. It was only later, during my more frequent interactions with him, that the full gamut of his many qualities became apparent. Sultan Ghalib, in spite of his numerous activities and involvement in many worthy causes and projects, took it upon himself to go over the manuscript with a fine-tooth comb, and very politely pointed out many areas of improvement and made valuable suggestions to improve the flow and readability. I am extremely grateful to him and cannot express my gratitude in mere words for his encouragement on my first effort at writing, and the time and effort he spent to bring the book to a higher level.

## Syed Babar Ali

Syed Babar Ali, OBE, is an entrepreneur and a philanthropist, with a deep passion for promoting Arts and Education, and for establishing Pakistan's leading business school, Lahore University of Management Sciences

From the time I met him in the early 80's, I have always found him to be soft-spoken down to earth, always imparting words of wisdom whenever we met. This wonderful person is an icon and a true mentor for my family and me. His worldly views and perspectives gave insight to my writing. I am indeed very fortunate that he kindly sent me a message for my book. My thanks are but a small tribute to him and his kindness.

## Prof. Deep Saini -Vice-Chancellor and President, University of Canberra, Australia.

Prof. Deep Saini, is a eminent scientist, visionary, and a powerhouse with a passion for promoting education.

I first met him when he graciously accepted my invitation to my art exhibition. He was then the Vice- President University of Toronto. Charismatic, articulate, and humble, this intellectual has inspired me, providing food for thought for my writing and by his outstanding accomplishments; at the same time making the Asian community proud. My special thanks to him; now a dear family friend, for taking time to write the lovely note for my book to be cherished by me forever, in spite of his important work responsibilities. His eloquent message with the fluidity of words is a reflection of his own personality.

# Thanks

My heartfelt thanks to Mr. Saqib Zia, Chairman Gillette Pakistan, and to Citizens Archive of Pakistan, for their help and granting permission to use copyright material. I am also thankful to Ms Stephanie A. Viereck Gibbs Kamnath, Assistant Professor University of Mass. Boston for granting permission to use the quote of Albert Einstein. Thanks also to Roger Koniski, ex IBM, for sharing the picture of Mont.St Micheal.

Special thanks to my dear friend, Saba Arshad, who was a source of encouragement and supported me all the way in my endeavors to write this memoir; from the birth of the idea of writing the book all the way to it being published.

To Aliya Shafi, Rashida Shoaib, and Komal Syed; for giving me the confidence to continue writing; after reading my first draft.

Thanks from the core of my heart to my dear children, Samir, Asim and Omar for always standing by me, and to their lovely wives Zareen, Sana and Gulrukh, in persuading me to write and for their continuous outpouring of love and support, and in being my help brigade in innumerable ways.

My very special thanks from the core of my heart, to my youngest son, Omar for helping me at all times and polishing my manuscript with his computer savvy skills and to his lovely and wonderful wife Gulrukh who was my sounding board and soul mate in grasping my vision and being forthright with her suggestions and printing my drafts.

Lastly a big thank you to my husband Imran, for being a pillar in my life journey, and for his unwavering support always, in all that I do. The existence of this book would certainly not have been possible without his suggestions and efforts in obtaining copyright permissions, correspondence with the publisher and much more.

# About the Author

In many ways, art gave birth to literature. The first stories written down were cave paintings, stone carvings and Arabesque. All these depicted the stories of people who lived before us. For years, drawings were the precursors of our alphabet, and the means to convey one's thoughts. This simply meant that the only people who could tell stories were those who could draw. Thus, a writer was essentially an artist.

Sabiha uses various art forms to do just that; expressing true passion, integrity, and transferring those emotions to her work. She draws deeply from her Eastern upbringing and philosophy, using the magic of the pen and brush to make it relevant to the Western eye; fusing East and West, spiritual and worldly, past and present, colors and thoughts, into something contemporary and relevant.

She has now harnessed the power of words to express the treasured all-encompassing real moments, and the insights from her life in her first book, "Tawafuq".

"Tawafuq" - not a coincidence, but a series of events that were all destined to come together; the people who shaped it, and those that helped her learn the true essence of compassion and spirituality, embracing all which was sensed and felt- strong enough to have stayed, and deserved to be shared alongside the naturally transcended wisdom.

Her paintings are supportive of the narrative and elaborate the prose with the same thoughts, duly enhancing their intrinsic nature.

Sabiha, a creative consultant and Interior Designer with a Commerce background, has held two solo shows; participated in many juried and joint exhibitions at a variety of venues, public and private. She also contributed to the first Canadian needlework art project; The Quilt of Belonging, exhibited at the Canadian Museum of Civilization, Ottawa and internationally.

# Preface

"If there's a book that you want to read,
but it hasn't been written yet, then you
must write it."
Toni Morrison

I had a keen desire to share my life's journey, its essence, and relevance; and to try to decipher the wisdom and coincidences behind some encounters that have shaped my life.

"There is no greater agony than bearing
an untold story inside you."
Maya Angelou

Over the years, I used to share with my family, some of the awe-inspiring conversations I had with my friends. I realized that these touched them deeply, more so as they had themselves known and interacted with them as they were growing up. This certainly added a sense of reality and relevance.

In a way, my children were imbibing the values and messages in these stories. On a number of occasions, they would tell me that I should write down these inspiring thoughts and anecdotes for them to have a broader resonance, so that some of the compassionate gestures and positive thoughts they conveyed may perchance be transferred.

Everything that happens in life is a story, your very own. I seriously contemplated, and loved the idea.

Knowing that I had not written earlier, I still had this desire to share these glimpses into the lives of the amazing compassionate people who have played a significant role in assisting me find my true self, while making a visible impact on the lives of others. For they are the ones who have influenced, mentored and polished my being, from a raw unfinished neophyte to a more complete person.

I wanted to evoke those same emotions; I myself had felt on experiencing them, and wish to share my lived-in vivid memories to subtly connect with the reader. Though not always easy finding the right words to create a level of bonding with those people the way I did.

This book is a medley of short stories: that of my emotions during times of grief and happiness; a portfolio of the moments of reality and unforgettable experiences in different chapters of my life. From being part of a family, to raising one's own; from travelling to diverse historically and culturally rich places to centers of pilgrimage; and into my innermost soul, trying to understand the meaning of life.

Along the way, many memorable moments and experiences were to cascade seamlessly through the sands of time.

I was to realize that these cherished, pleasant and enriching encounters on most occasions of pure serendipity, seemingly random and unrelated, were gradually to appear not just mere coincidences, but were 'Meant to be'. In hindsight, they formed a very coherent thread, which had plenty a role in bringing me closer to the light within, as each one of us has a soul connection with the Divine.

Although the perceptions of the philosophy of Islam, does influence me deeply, due to my personal background, belief and individual experiences, I do strongly believe that spirituality goes across and beyond all sects, castes, and religion.

In the Rubaiyat, the 11th century Persian philosopher-poet Omar Khayyam writes,

> "The Moving Finger writes; and, having writ,
> Moves on: Nor all thy Piety nor Wit
> Shall lure it back to cancel half a line;
> Nor all thy Tears wash out a Word of it."
> Translation by Edward FitzGerald

Some have understood these verses to mean that whatever one does in one's life, is one's own responsibility and cannot be changed; while others interpret it to mean, that our journey and destination is preordained, even while having been given freedom of choice.

One realization that struck me while writing this book is the insignificance of one's self in context of the vast universe; and the pleasure and fulfilment one gets from helping others.

The Arabic word "Tawafuq" explains my journey very well. As the word means, it is not just coincidence but was destined and 'meant to be'.

I decided on the title of my book after some deep thought and reflection. In reality, the decision itself is a perfect example of 'Tawafuq'.

I came across the word while on a visit to Cairo, where I stumbled upon a poster while parking my car. I had never before come across this word, and somehow it intrigued me to no end.

However, on further research and study, I realized that the word 'Tawafuq', has a much deeper and even a mystical meaning and connotation.

The word 'Tawafuq' is something that connotes balance, harmony, and a certain order. Whereas both 'Coincidence' and 'Serendipity' allude to the fact, that something happened by chance.

The whole universe, as a creation, operates on and is a perfect example of 'Tawafuq', everything in place and in perfect harmony and balance; each component designed and "Meant to be".

My life and my path to the title again is how events are closely related and planned by the Creator Himself.

Saadi Shirazi, the Persian poet of the medieval period and regarded as the poet of love and compassion writes,

"My companions' virtues elevated me,
I am otherwise the same humble creature."

My painting below encompasses the enriching encounters with enlightened souls, which were not mere coincidences, but 'Meant to be'. We meet many people, but only a few make a difference in our lives.

Sabiha Imran
Toronto 2019

**My Journey**

# THE EARLY YEARS

Every year, on the night of August 14$^{th}$, the independence day of Pakistan, there is widespread jubilation; the skies light up with fireworks as the crowds celebrate the independence from the British Raj and the birth of a sovereign nation. This is a historic moment, a moment that created a safe haven for people with different cultures and ethnic backgrounds; and to become a common denominator for these people, to share and unite them.

The flag raising ceremonies, parades, and crowds of people make this a momentous day every year; bringing people together from near and far to express gratitude and pay tribute to the motherland.

It was on this auspicious night, much later after the partition, that my mother gave birth to me, completing our small and happy family.

I enjoyed a very pleasant and simple childhood; but times were hard indeed for many of the families who had migrated. One can only begin to understand and relate to the magnitude, change and travails of these people affected, by listening to some of their true stories.

Fayyazi and Mahmud Minhas, my mother and father, lovingly called *Ammijan* and *Abbijan* by us, were amongst the very few lucky to escape the upheaval; and with difficulty managed to get on board a train for the newly created Pakistan. They were part of the crowd in the train which was crowded with so many others fleeing from the violence and mayhem. They boarded the coach with the newborn; my older twin brothers making the journey from Simla, the summer capital of the British raj to Karachi. I had been hearing about this hill station from them and their wonderful life in it ever since I was a child, making it sound like it was no less than paradise.

The British choose this picturesque hill station, built on top of seven hills, to escape from the oppressive heat and summers of the winter capital, Delhi. This allowed them respite and a chance to relax and enjoy the bracing climate, which they imagined to have reminded them of home.

To the Indo-Victorian Nobel Laureate, Rudyard Kipling, "It was a centre of power as well as pleasure."

The partition was traumatic for the sub continent. People settled for generations in their native ancestral homes had to flee from the familiar environs to safety across the freshly drawn borders.

They had to abandon their homes, their rightful domains, big or small, with their entire belongings. In most cases, these sanctuaries were the only assets they owned, in a place they thought they would be dwelling in forever.

This was a time, when nothing else mattered, except their lives, with a fear of the unknown looming over their heads. No one knew what the future held, as riots were erupting and flaring in different parts of the country.

Amidst the chaos, pandemonium and panic crowned by an overbearing fear were grim faces with blank expressions at the station, even as they held on to their dear ones, the children crying and cringing with fear; the elderly, barely able to walk and tightly holding on to any support and all seemingly drowned in a river of uncertainty. The ripples of reality were in a constant state of flux: it was the ultimate hope for the much-awaited change for a better life.

Needless to add, they were all to end up with bitter memories about the uprooting and migration.

My parents though still carried a compassionate heart wherever they went.

Forced by circumstances to leave a settled life and their ties with family and friends behind, under extraordinary circumstances, they had hardly been able to carry just the essentials with many resorted to novel stratagems to do so. Ammi wore a number of shirts one over the other, while the children's clothes had been stuffed into a small pillow.

My father's Sikh Indian colleague offered to safeguard their possessions that were left behind, consoling and assuring him that he will look after, and hold them in trust for him until he came back.

Once, this person - the epitome of true friendship - saw my mother's hand embroidered panels, and a floral arrangement, made out of fish scales which he had seen her sanding and polish.; were being sold in one of the shops. He felt very disturbed and bought them, sad that the pieces so lovingly created were on sale, with the intention of returning them back to their creator and the owner of these masterpieces.

My father always reminisced about this man's goodness with great reverence.

Ammijan and Abbijan, then a young couple, started to a build their new life after partition, in the emerging capital port city of Karachi. This city of lights is said to have been founded in 1729; however this region was known much earlier to the Arabs as early as 712 C.E, due to the route that they followed in trade with then, Ceylon.

The partition was a catastrophe in so many ways, as thousands of refugees kept entering Pakistan and India through the Pak-Indo borders, and is considered the largest forced migration in world history. In the aftermath of partition, migrants were struggling with economic instability and lack of resources to sustain their families. The world had tumbled over for them. Many immigrants were placed in barracks, shelters and temporary camps, until the time, they were shifted to better places. In the after-effects of war, there are many similar instances; one which I recall are the Selimiye Turkish Army barracks in Istanbul, converted at the time of Crimean War in-1854, into a Military hospital under the care of Florence Nightingale, who is credited for laying the foundations for the noble Nursing profession. Napier barracks, as we all remember growing up in Karachi, were named after Sir Charles Napier, the first governor of Sind, and Jacob lines after General John Jacob. During this time, lifetime friendships were formed with some refugee neighbours, as all shared similar plight. My parents, though somewhat settled, in that new unsettled phase, felt a strong natural commitment to help other fellow refugees as best as possible. Even at that difficult juncture in their lives, they helped wherever they could, as this was their second nature. It may not have been in kind, but in every other way possible; guiding all in need, and in their struggle for survival; suggesting potential venues of employment to find their feet in a new country. They helped families register their children in schools, for in many cases, most male members had been unable to accompany their families.

I kept hearing about their experiences and out of the way gestures from various sources when I grew up. In short, this dignified, unassuming duo were a godmother and godfather to many.

Their experiences of going through this painful trauma and the highly testing times, had also added to their deep sense of innate compassion.

Most of my childhood was spent during the military regime of Ayub Khan in the sixties, the second President of Pakistan, a phase regarded by some as 'The greatest decade' in the history of the country.

For Pakistan, rich in resources had begun to flourish economically, and with it, everyone's financial conditions, including ours began to improve.

Ammijan and Abbijan gave us everything; sometimes at a great sacrifice to themselves. They were people extraordinaire! We did not have a home filled with material things, but the warmth and love that exuded from this home was enough to attract people from far and near.

"This was a rose garden from our house
to the rose garden in our hearts; for a
fragrance that will not diminish".
Unknown

Our "House on the Prairie" was in the midst of a metropolitan city, yet "Far from the Madding Crowd."

My mother, without any formal education was one of the world's great, undiscovered gem; and an example of old-world charm - a 'Limited edition'; the kind and breed that is not produced any more. She was always showering her kindness and wisdom on everyone, inspiring and enriching them by her mere presence and personality - Here was a woman who led a simple life, but one enriched with noble thoughts, ideals, and selfless deeds.

My three older brothers and I had been brought-up in an atmosphere, which was to instill in us values, all which we came to appreciate and cherish forever.

With the morning dew, fresh breeze, and bright sunshine, we woke up to a radiant dawn, with the cat purring away on seeing the four musketeers awake. Oh! However, there was no time to cuddle her. It was our rotating duty to change her water and brush this beautiful Himalayan feline's coat. Without wasting time, she would display an obvious attitude.

Four pressed, starched white uniforms lined our corridor; all in a line with white socks and polished sneakers. A warm breakfast awaited us; eggs and toast with a glass of hot milk. Our lunch boxes were lovingly packed.

All this conducted and orchestrated by an unbelievably perfectionist woman who made everything sing and dance in order. Gleefully we marched out of the house with the right chords of happiness and singing;

"Lub pay aatee hay dua, bun kay tamanna mairee"
(Our hearts desire comes to our lips as a prayer)

This is an inspiring poem in Urdu, by the great poet-philosopher of the East, Allama Iqbal. It is a prayer seeking compassionate qualities and a desire to serve humanity. The title 'Allama', is used in reference to a great scholar.

Iqbal's poetry influenced me even more; mainly due to his connection with my grandfather, Aziz Minhas, who was a contemporary and colleague of his.

**My painting inspired by Iqbal's famous verses on 'Khudi' (Self) and 'Hasti' (Existence)**

We were nurtured in a household where caring and giving were a way of life.

Going back in time to incidents of my childhood filled with incredible memories, I recall that one afternoon as we returned from school, loaded with homework and empty lunch boxes; we saw grave anxiety and unease on Ammi's face; she was holding a stack of food containers, and appeared greatly anxious to leave. She told us that she is disturbed, as a distant relative; a widow with six children, who had recently migrated to Pakistan and, had been devastated by a series of unfortunate experiences was struggling to support her children and manage her household. Hence, as usual, my mother's innate goodness prompted her to do her bit in lessening the burdens of her relative as best as she could.

Every morning, since then, while I was at school, she would prepare meals for that family, and delivered it to them, using public transport or whatever means she could find, always ensuring to arrive back home before us.

Punctuality and perfection were an important part of Ammi's life. The set schedule for us was to finish our homework before Abbi came back from work. In spite of her watchful eye, we often managed to disturb this rhythm by clandestinely sneaking out of our rooms undetected. One of us would volunteer to keep a vigilant watch and warn us in good time about Abbi's return from office by listening for the sound of the opening of the latch of the house gate. This was like an alarm system, heralding that Abbi had arrived.

Upon this, we would do a swift dash towards our desks and appear glued to our books. This long desk, made by our father accommodated all four of us. The sight that his children were studying hard gave him immense pleasure and our ruse worked often.

There was always an air of anticipation as we presented our report cards. The 'A' grades certainly paid off by earning us the reward of being allowed to eat our favourite cream rolls from the Pereira Bakery, the then famous confectioners in Karachi.

The fun was in the fact that we would indulge in these adventures of ours, while Ammi would be in the adjacent room seen sitting on a stool, sewing on her favourite hand operated and foot pedalled Singer machine. This ever-faithful machine is still cherished, as an heirloom in our family.

As far as I can remember; until I started stitching myself, Ammi would lovingly design and stitch my clothes. Her work was always as detailed and neat at the back as it was on the front.

**The Heirlooms - My Mother's Embroideries**

My brother Arif, once got a big surprise as he was leaving for the airport, when she put on him a cardigan that she had started knitting just a day earlier.

One of her friends, Mrs. Wajid Khan, who was working for the government in the social work sector, knowing her compassionate nature and myriad extraordinary talents, requested her to volunteer and teach at various centers. She willingly agreed, and with great love, imparted these talents to many young women, so that they could earn a living, working from their homes.

I grew up seeing, but realizing only much later, my mother's subtle ways in empowering people around her, nurturing them, while understanding their talents and needs. Ammijan blossomed in so many amazing ways, dedicated to changing lives and giving hope and courage to so many.

Begum I. A. Khan, wife of the Joint Secretary, Establishment Division, O & M Wing photographed with the committee members of the Central Government Staff Welfare Ladies Industrial Home, Jacob Lines at the prize distribution function. Front row (from right) are: Mrs. Mirza, Mrs. Minhas, Mrs. Wajid Khan (Staff Welfare Officer), chief guest, and Mrs. Shanul Haq Haqqi, Chairman of the Centre.

**Ammijan, 2nd from right, front row with Mrs Wajid Khan**

**Begum Raana Liaquat Ali Khan inaugurated an industrial home in Jacob Lines on Saturday. Picture shows Begum Sahiba at a stall.—("News" photo).**

**Ammijan, with Begum Liaqat Ali Khan, wife of the
first Prime Minister of Pakistan**

When the month of fasting approached, Ammi would go and get bolts of fabric, which she gifted to deserving families, so that they too could celebrate Eid and enjoy this auspicious day, wearing new clothes. She religiously followed this gesture every year.

Indeed, very soon, my mother was to become a mother to all of them, loved and appreciated by all.

Those were the days when readymade garments were still not available. Later she was to go with my father to buy sewing machines, which she proceeded to gift to them.

I was fortunate indeed to be the daughter of this great man; an epitome of dignity, unpretentious, generous and loving to everyone he met; He was unquestionably the best person I knew or will ever know, and a favourite with all; the poor, the rich, the young and the old alike, and in every strata of the society.

My father had the honour of being a Ravian, an alumni of the Govt. College University; the oldest institution in the Indo-Pak Subcontinent, founded in 1864 and which is proud to have produced some notable alumni and Nobel laureates. He loved Lahore and his inherited association with it, and would enjoy saying "Lahore, Lahore hai", while immediately switching to Punjabi with his siblings. As my mother with a refined Urdu speaking background, hailed from Agra, the home of the Taj Mahal, the symbol of and a tribute to love, fidelity, and faithfulness. Their union itself was the result of the friendship of my maternal and paternal grand fathers, who loved and respected each other immensely.

Abbi had a delightful way of conversation that fostered and nurtured friendships easily. He enjoyed sharing his wisdom and would narrate stories of his life with enthusiasm, as if reliving them, and with every word and anecdote full of wit. It was a pleasant way of remembering his yester years.

I remember few of these vividly, as they are very strongly etched in my mind.

Every now and then, Shabbir bhai casually dropped in to visit our father, simply to pay his respects. He was a simple rickshaw driver, a good man in his early fifties, who had the burden of responsibility of his old mother and his own family of four.

He would sit with my father, both with teacups in their hands, in the covered porch of our house, reverently kept listening to my father's advice with a lowered gaze.

My parents would also visit his family occasionally; and without making it obvious took care of them. We later found out that they had bought a taxicab for him to earn a better living.

Abbijan's helpful nature and the garden kept him occupied and never let him retire. Being an avid gardener, he nurtured his plants with love. Of all his plants, roses were his favourite.

It was many years later that I learned that there is much more that meets the eye, in the transformation of a small bud to a fully blossomed flower - our life's cycle from birth to maturity.

"There is simply the rose; it is perfect
in every moment of its existence."
R.W. Emerson

In the early fifties, Pakistan, a new country was lacking in infrastructure and basic facilities. As in every other sector, this shortage also affected the government hospitals.

Abbijan, in keeping with his nature, could not bear to see anyone in despair, and would channel all his resources to help in any manner possible. Certain memories remain with me in this regard, which have made an indelible impact on our lives.

Once an acquaintance of his had a severe infection, causing multiple organ failure and which came to the point that they had to amputate the leg. Abbi used to be with him and his family in the hospital so that he could keep abreast with his friend's condition in-order to consulting more doctors. He would also arrange for the medications that were not available then through different means. Luckily with proper care and over a period, his condition had started to improve. We could only sense our father's relief later.

As seen, Ammijan and Abbijan not only managed their own lives, but also went out of their way to help other lives in need, wherever and whenever they were and at the same time teaching us the value of truth and perseverance. I was a witness to their compassion towards all and sundry.

More than anything what stood out and which I now recognize years later is that there was the aura of 'Inner light' within them - the simplicity, humility, and warmth with which they raised us and embraced others. It makes me realize and appreciate their dedication and steady perseverance in our upbringing, and placing great emphasis on our education, as they believed, that there is nothing compared to it.

They made sacrifices that only a parent would make for his children, putting everything aside, to send us to reputable schools. The environment at St.Joseph's Convent school and college, my 'Alma mater', a term so beautifully expressed in Latin - Soul mother, was much like at home. 'Modesty is a virtue', was almost a mantra. Alongside, with those core values, our generation held deep respect for elders and especially for our teachers. They were almost like a second set of parents, moulding the girls in our school as the mothers and leaders of tomorrow.

**In the St. Joseph Convent School Courtyard, established in 1862;
with Sister Terezina, its Principal at the time.**

**By courtesy of Citizens Archive Pakistan**

Even back then in Pakistan, many people were enlightened and educated their daughters. An aura of simplicity prevailed in our land of five rivers; which is blessed so richly with a landscape of beautiful colours and textures of many a hue.

It was this nurturing of values, and the "Do-it-yourself" attitude in this motivating environment which those teachings instilled, that was to leave an eternal impact, and serve us so well throughout our lives by becoming an important part of our being, always reminding us, of who we are and what we can become.

John Dewey has expressed these sentiments aptly indeed by stating;

> "Education is not preparation for life.
> Education is life itself."

Even though, I was never told directly to love God, yet, it is this genuine and dedicated love for Him and for humanity that I had learnt and which has always guided me on the right path in life. I became cognizant of those simple and wholesome teachings, though not formally taught to me in a religious context but instilled quietly in me with love, as the real core teachings of any religion.

Religion and love for God transcend across all cultures and boundaries. This was all the more evident to us living in a post-partitioned country with Muslims, Hindus, Sikhs and Christians, living side by side in peace and harmony.

> "The good life is one inspired by love and
> guided by knowledge."
> Bertrand Russel

Though I did not realize at the time, much of my artwork displayed the emotions I had experienced earlier. However, it was gradually to dawn on me over the years, that I was transferring these inner feelings onto the canvas when using my brush.

The compassion and goodness that I witnessed in my parents, was later over the years to be noticeable in many others, as mirrored images, leaving ever so subtly an imprint, conducive of changing one's life's perspective.

Indeed, it would only be apt to say that one realizes over a period, that life is an adventurous journey, to be loved, experienced, enjoyed, and shared with others.

As now, I too begin to share some impressionable moments encountered and which were not mere coincidences but were 'meant to be', with different people, in completely different places and at different times, yet - all stories though being so different, are braided together with a common thread of shared goodness.

# LIFE, 'WELL' - LIVED

This was a simple excursion trip to a mango grove, turning out to be an adventure, where, we were a mere conduit to this man, who created resonance in a remote land, by his single act.

In Pakistan, people eagerly await the festive mango season, which comes in full zest and lasts from May until August. This fruit's exotic tropical aroma, wafting through air, is tantalizing to the senses and titillating to the taste buds. It is seen everywhere, from kitchens, to drawing rooms, from roadside intersections to narrow alleys, and most popularly, in carts under the shade of trees. This king of fruits, which resides in our hearts, has a love affair with all, at first sight, and first bite.

The sweet fragrance of this yellow sunshine fruit is ubiquitous. They have the power to intoxicate the flies too; whirling and twirling in ecstasy as the aroma from these mangos is beyond temptation. Well, these mangoes call for another stimulating discussion over a cup of tea.

Our neighbors had a mango farm in Sindh, Pakistan. This area has the Thar Desert in the East, the Kirthar Mountains to the West, dividing Sindh from Balochistan, and the Arabian Sea to the South.

The Sindh province having its roots deep in history and has been the centre of the Indus Valley Civilization, which had flourished more than five thousand years ago. Some old ruins are still seen basking in the sun; as if a testimony to the past. Due to its proximity to the mighty Indus River, farming settlements had begun to be visible then. Later around 1800 BC, the decline of the civilization started to appear, as the theory suggests is due to climate change, resulting in the disrupted river ecosystems.

'Bhai Sahib', as he was known in the neighborhood, generously and lovingly gave a crate of 'Chaunsa' mangoes to us every season. This variety had acquired its name from the commemoration of the victory by Emperor Sher Shah Suri, in the year 1539, over Mughal Emperor Humayun at Chaunsa.

They had invited us many times to their farm for mango picking.

Who could refuse this tempting offer! Finally, one weekend we all packed into our Range Rover following their grey sedan, Peugeot, for an exciting trip to the mango grove,. Since these remote areas do not have any signposts, they gave us a few landmarks to follow in case we miss each other, which we unfortunately did. After turning away from the highway, we lost sight of their vehicle. As now, we had to follow the directions, they had casually mentioned.

Right turn from the few mud dwellings, go straight, and make another u-turn from the thorny tall bushes, then continue twenty meters straight, that leads directly to their grove.

This simple direction seemed easy to follow, but after a visibly steep incline, it was like advancing to no-man's land.

This entire route was clearly setting the stage for a rollercoaster ride. Sandy bumpy road for the most part, made us feel we were galloping on a horse, in this wild open arena of nowhere.

Continuing further on our way, we were delighted to see the 'Truck Adda', a place of rest for the weary truck drivers, and a much needed, respite for us at that point. The Adda was full of life, blaring folk music in full volume, though unsure where the sound was coming from, the cigarette shop or the nearby petrol station.

Few trucks lined on each side of the lively little restaurant, becoming a timely screen for the drivers, comfortably lounging on tightly stretched, wooden charpoys, weaved artistically, with coloured jute rope. Relaxing and sipping tea after a monotonous, long haul. The strong concoction of the tea, determines the mileage they still have to undertake, to keep them awake.

These were the days when the GPS and cell phones did not exist, which often made navigation a challenge.

We lost track of the grey Peugeot, which might have turned sandy grey within a period of three hours. For sure, it will be light brown, by the time it reaches its destination, just like ours. If one wants a quick color transformation, this was the place to go. The beauty that is forced on you is inevitable, a hallmark of this environment.

Driving on this path had turned it into almost a formal road, just by the little traffic that it has to endure by the inhabitants of this remote land.

As expected, there were no signs, only certain God given landmarks for people of wisdom to discern and follow. We did not know where we were and simultaneously where we were heading.

Furthermore, to make matters more interesting, the car heated up, as if in profuse display of its deep frustrated anger.

There was also no water in sight. The Little Bo-Peep in me noticed a few thatched mud houses in this barren land. We had to have trust in God and beg for help.

Our search was interrupted by a melodious sound floating in the air. On close listening, I realized that it was the sound of someone playing the Alghoza flute. The melody was so soulful and enchanting that it permeated the plains of this wilderness. This felt like a live concert just for us!

The lyrical melody of this well-known Sufi song "Dhama dhum Mast Qalandar" simply captivated our hearts. This alluring, spiritual song is a tribute by a famous sufi poet, Amir Khusrow composed in honour of the revered sufi saint Lal Shahbaz Qalandar, referred also as 'Jhulelal'.

The whole nation loves this song, and every generation listens to it with joy ever since its composition.

As the transcendent sound became insistent, we knelt down and tried to become comfortable, sitting cross-legged on the sandy barren ground. Our muscles after a short while showed signs of strain, as they had not been used to this posture since sometime.

When the mellow musical melody grew much clearer, we saw a middle-aged man approaching, his frail shoulders covered in an 'Ajrak', the traditional, maroon shawl indicating, even from far his deep connection to the Sindhi heritage. The Sindhi's proudly wear this- not deemed a status symbol in this entire region.

The sight of his attire gave us an instant feeling of comfort. While still unsure of his knowing this area, we all started imagining and expecting some help.

Approaching us, it was noticeable that this man is a little apprehensive and concerned and confused at our presence in this Empty Quarter. He sat down visibly tired, his pleated loose pants clearly displayed signs of having once being white. With a salt and pepper mustache, spanning the width of his face and with piercing eyes, he looked first at the Range Rover, later glanced at us. The look was half-sympathetic and a quarter suspicious; as many stories involving banditry were in circulation then, maybe the case even now.

We requested him to play a few old melodies. With a slight pause, he recited a beautiful poem by Hazrat Sachal Sarmast, another famous mystic poet from Sindh, who had the distinction of writing poetry, in seven languages, (number seven again) encompassing pure Divine love and his belief in unity of existence. This man clearly seemed to enjoy sharing his passion with us, and appearing visibly happy to have an appreciative audience at that time, in the middle of this dessert. This experience was so uplifting, that our tension simply evaporated; as I reminiscence my visit as a child from Hyderabad (Sindh) to Sehwan with my family. It was probably an hour and a half drive, but clearly, a long journey for a child, through a barren range of hills. All I remember is the sweltering heat, glittering mirrors and colourful tiles, and a courtyard full of people with an attitude of deep respect.

This nomad was in Sehwan Sharif just for a short time, where the revered Sufi saint, Lal Shahbaz Qalandar, believed to be a contemporary of Rumi, came to enlighten this area of Sind. Almost since the 13th century, this whole area is famous for saints and mystics, who settled there to preach peace and unity.

While availing this God given opportunity of friendship, we inquired about water from this nomad. This simple chemical combination of $H_2O$, was difficult to find. The latter part was certainly there, as proved by our very existence.

He asked us to accompany him to his dwellings, which were just a few kilometers away.

Undertaking this necessary journey, would still mean that there would only be some water to drink and for nothing else.

Meanwhile, our host, worried at having lost sight of our car, had also sent a rescue team to locate us. In hindsight, this unpaved road was to prove to be a blessing for us as well the search party. For they were able to follow the marks left by our Range Rover. It was so quiet in this desert environment, that any car driving past in this close vicinity, echoed and resonated, almost like the sound of the thunder. Reminding us of our family's ancient alarm clock, whose unpleasant loud sound one could not ignore. Our excitement at seeing the car was indescribable. Both were relieved at seeing each other.

We were thus safely to arrive at the grove, with some time to enjoy the mango picking before the glorious sunset in this otherwise dry empty arid land; that lacked stimulus completely.

Sunsets and sunrise, do not shy from displaying their magical beauty, even in an empty desert, nor behind the mountains or on the oceans, never failing to disappear and emerge in a most breathtaking, enchanting way. One helps us to sleep; the other wakes us up. This play of dawn to dusk has been there from time unknown and will continue until time unknown.

However, before parting from our nomad host, we had a little chat. He very candidly described the scarcity of water in this area, which often led them to lead a semi-nomadic life, who though free in spirit, had to wander about to satisfy their basic needs.

Their women were the lifeline of the family. It was so upsetting to know their responsibility to fetch the water. The young children, despite their tender age, have no choice, but to accompany the mother in this scorching heat. These children went through this monotonous, uninteresting journey of almost 4-6 hours each day. The women are simply able to fetch 50-60 liters of water on a trip, holding two clay pots one placed on their head, the other one in their arms, a balancing act of sorts.

Sadly, to add to this daily ordeal, they also often had to face droughts in this arid area; and it seemed they have not seen anything better. I stood there thinking about these people, as they too must be having some hope, some aspirations in their lives to move on, as this is the unfortunate life they have seen and led since the time of their birth.

Once in a while when it rains, they collect the rainwater to maintain their, the so called kitchen garden for self-sustenance during those harsh months that can sometimes lead them to famine. The water that they collect from the well is at times not fit for human consumption.

It was heartbreaking to hear the life that they lead in such distressing situations. Our excitement of picking the mangoes faded, as we kept thinking, that the daily basic necessities of life, taken for granted by us, are their very basic, essential necessities that they need so badly for survival.

The hardships endured by them, are certainly lamentable. Their yesterdays are almost, always similar to their tomorrows. Not knowing what their future is likely to be, they simply do not nurture expectation for it.

For a few years after that, we lost touch with Bhai Sahib and his family, as they had sold their house and moved from our neighborhood. Meanwhile, their children and we, all were married and moved to different parts of the world. Yet whenever the mango season approached, we remembered them with great affection.

Coincidentally, we were once to meet his eldest son with whom we enjoyed a very stimulating conversation, which of course was to include our fondness for the highly regarded, exotic, and delectable mangoes; and the days gone by.

Eating mangoes has always been a delight for me. As a child, I had found that it was best to enjoy them alone, as the gooey juice sometimes sneak, through your fingers to travel south, towards the elbows, without stopping, and still wanting more!

We had learnt that they had sold half their farm, when their father had come to realize that in their parallel, neighboring land, people were living in such deplorable conditions.

He had thought the same, like President Obama once said, "They're not very different or unusual from us, nor less worthy", hence it was time for him to stand up for these isolated people, and get them out of this miserable situation.

Bhai Sahib had to go the conventional way, with a team of people. In order to establish the availability of water, they had to insert probes into the ground. This was not only to measure the water level but also to ensure that the water is sweet for drinking, or saline for other use. The challenges were phenomenal; drilling through hard rock, in search of plain water, almost to the depths of 400 feet below the surface.

Now this roaring drilling sound, that permeated the quite environment; started to amplify in installments.

Upon hearing this commotion and witnessing the digging from far, a dweller who walked with great effort, supporting himself at every step had approached them with two young boys, in clear bewilderment.

This old man, speaking in a frail voice and Sindhi accent, inquired of them if they were planning to dig a well in this location.

He informed them, that as previously, there had been a well here. However, while they were away, searching for food and water, during the drought months, they were shocked upon their return to find that the well was closed, filled with sand and rocks. This source of water, they had all benefited from the well in the past, had gone forever.

The man had lived and struggled, in this area, most of his life. His white beard and deep lines on his face, clearly displayed the years of exposure to the harsh elements of this agonizing environment.

Upon hearing this, Bhai Sahib ordered the workers to dig the same spot pointed by him and where their gauge too, was showing a reservoir of water underneath.

As they began excavating the site of the well, just a few meters underneath, they saw some boxes in the rubble. That was strange! The workers lifted the heavy boxes to the surface. All curious to know what was inside. As they opened one box, they were completely shocked and surprised to see them filled with gold and silver jewellery, as well as other valuables.

To us, listening to this tale was like reliving the story of an episode of Ali Baba and the forty thieves.

The workers, and all those present there had actually seen and experienced the realization of this unique legend, which they once must have listened.

Tradition has it that during the 1947 partition of India and Pakistan, there was chaos and uncertainty. Hindus and Sikhs fled to India from Pakistan, and Muslims vice versa to Pakistan from India. Disorder prevailed. Refugees were attacked, and many looted during those unforeseen riots. This was a time where people were trying to save their lives, abandoning all their belongings they felt could prove an impediment on their journey. They buried their belongings, in the hope that they might be able to come back, and perchance still find them. The safest place they thought was to bury it in the ground.

At that time Muslim families who had migrated from India, claimed many houses in Sind, in lieu of their homes they had left behind. Later, when people lived in those claimed houses, many residents had found valuables buried inside their new homes.

Astonished and mesmerized at seeing this hidden treasure, they did not know how to react to this unexpected development. After careful consideration, they consulted responsible people of the 'Tehsil', (Administrative division of an area) and mutually with their local clan, and they came up with a few options that would be beneficial to this area in the future, and benefit all those that live there.

The excavation of the well continued, cleaned and brought back to its full pristine glory. Also encouraged by this success, they dug up a few more wells, in areas close to their dwellings. The families, specially the women, were overwhelmed with joy as it made their daily task so much easier.

Bhai Sahib's son shared with us a small video clip, showing all of them rejoicing, singing in ecstasy, the famous Sindhi folk song, 'Ho Jamalo'.

He told us a very interesting legend, which he believed is the origin of this song. I had loved it mainly because of its upbeat rhythm, but hearing the story, I have to come to enjoy it even more.

With the lyrics resonating in my head, he joyfully shared. "During the British era in 1889 Lansdowne Bridge in Sukkur, Sindh province was completed. This steel bridge on River Indus had been built for the trains to pass; but had not been tested yet. It is believed, to resolve the matter, the then government started training Sukkur jail prisoners, and told them that whoever test-drives the train across the bridge would be released. A man named Jamalo agreed to do so, to guarantee his release, if he crossed these two cities safely from Sukkur across to Rohri. Jamalo luckily was able to accomplish it and then was freed. His wife had then composed this song on his triumph; for a man with a brave heart, and complete faith. To me, however, his story did not hold any logic, as the engineers must have calculated the risk, rather than ask the prisoners to test drive. While still some think, to encounter against certain invaders, Jamalo came out victorious. Whichever is true, this folk song certainly puts people in a cheerful swaying mood.

This legend and many other similar romantic and poignant love stories of people from diverse lands, carrying additionally with them the regional and cultural differences are a testament to their unwavering emotional and Divine love, without its borders, or boundaries. As their tragic romances, love and bond is narrated so richly, it convinces itself to be real, than to believe, they are simply folklore and unauthenticated. These legends are part of the grand five thousand year old historical past, which connect these timeless mystical stories, all distinct yet separate, in the same manner of Punjab's five river tributaries, all merging together to gracefully flow into the mighty Indus. Likewise, linking these tales, through those mountains where the Aryans entered, deserts encountered by the Arabs, a land that attracted the saints, the armies and generals and its plains where Alexander made its way.

With the 'Ho Jamalo' song still in the background, he mentioned that his father formed a trust; the money from the treasure trove was availed to develop a clinic and school.

Once, in a while, one member of Bhai Sahib's family visits this place to ensure that everything is going smoothly, and taken care of by the people living there. By giving the shared responsibility to the dwellers of the village, Bhai Sahib had provided them the opportunity to manage and take care of their own resources, with a huge sense of responsibility, pride, and accountability.

Listening to his son, I think with Bhai Sahib's dedication, perseverance, and good intentions; unanticipated, positive events must have continued to happen. A single act by him had resonated in this cascading effect of alleviating the problems he saw in his neighbouring land. He wholeheartedly went on a mission to eradicate their sufferings and with his great effort, he was able to overcome the challenges these people faced in times of adversity.

We almost live in our bubble, often unaware of the realities of the world around us. This trip had made me witness their miserable circumstances of the people of the area, completely by chance. I was to discover that this and some similar experiences were gradually making me more sensitive, with the softer side of me taking over.

This tale captures in lucid terms, the true essence of compassion.

# THE JOURNEY BEGINS

Pakistan late 70's

After my wonderful childhood days, I got married soon after my graduation into a family that introduced me to an eclectic mix of accomplished and spiritual individuals. Their lineage and heritage connected to very learned and respected members, some connected with Royalty, in that they were Ministers in the inner circle of the court of the Nawab of Bhopal. Established by a Pashtun soldier, this Indian princely state had the distinction of having been ruled successfully for almost a century by four progressive women, popularly known as the Begums of Bhopal.

Bhopal is also widely known as the "City of lakes." It is built on seven hills and with its lakes, some depicting it as picturesque as the seventh heaven.

Interestingly, the many occurrences of number seven continues to fascinate me.

Being the youngest in my family and theirs as well, the simple rule for a young new bride was to love and respect everyone; which to me came naturally. In return, they admired and reciprocated this simple gesture generously. With some, the relationship has been phenomenal.

The elders who loved me and made me feel part of the family are now sadly no more in this world, leaving many a moment and instances of profound memories.

Among the many distinguished members of the family and friends that I met was Mahfooz Uncle, my father-in-law's friend. He must have been in his seventies, a dignified, spiritual person with a very distinct radiance on his face. His appearance was such that its magnetic appeal instantly drew me to him and I felt a mysterious connection and bond. Though his voice was frail, it never the less carried a sense of great strength; and one was mesmerized as one listened to him. His words reverberated in my heart and seemed to carry a message as if especially meant for me.

Grey hair covered his pale, olive face, with hazy, piercing eyes. However the overriding message that exuded from his personality was one of love and compassion.

Whenever we visited him, I found him comfortably ensconced in his Bombay rosewood recliner. The sight of this chair charmed me every time. His possession of this piece of furniture was from the era of the British Raj, as he too originally hailed from Bombay. A connoisseur or art aficionado would certainly have fallen in love with this chair. Its heritage linked to the Parsi community, who were pioneers of the furniture trade in Bombay at that time.

I too, quietly picked up my chair and placed it in a position where uncle could see me without craning his head. During our conversation, he would often slip in some words or thoughts that carried great wisdom yet in a way were just common sense.

With his laboured breathing, he lovingly addressed me, "I am so happy that you are now a member of the family and carrying its traditions forward". "I know that you will enjoy your role as a wife, mother, and daughter; but also try to be aware and conscious of the universal duty towards humanity."

Those words of his, not only had a profound impact on me at that instant, but also have stayed on with me in my mind and soul since that time.

This realization struck me again, almost forty years later, while attending a lecture by Payam Akhavan, a leading international lawyer and a professor at McGill University. He was conveying the same message, but in different words which seemed more relevant in today's troubled and materialistic world. "You need genuine empathy, the capacity to feel the pain of others, to experience an intimate shared humanity, to accept discomfort and sacrifice in the path of the greater cause", was how the Professor had expressed the same on this occasion.

Whenever I visited Mahfooz Uncle, I observed during our conversation, that while resting his hands on his lap, he would be constantly moving his index finger, almost as if writing something. The movement was obvious and repetitive.

I was quite intrigued on noticing this peculiar movement and could not resist asking him about it, though I was initially hesitant and felt reluctant to do so. However, my curiosity despite the sensitivity of this issue made me enquire about the significance of this action..

I was in awe of his reply. He glanced at me and responded in a whisper in an ethereal voice.

"I write the word 'God', which keeps me reminded with every breath of the Divine presence." I listened to him with attention, though the significance of it did not sink in me at that young age.

His mind and body always seemed to be synchronized beautifully in 'Zikr', the state of the remembrance of God, which is the echo and a deep synthesis of our whole being.

Those were his retirement days.

On a sunny, quiet, humid afternoon, I visited uncle again. Being alone and not keeping too well, uncle had left his house, and was living then in a modest place with his cousin.

The house was in a busy alley teeming with youngsters. They were playing cricket, which in Pakistan is a passion and the favourite sport of the young and old. Our country has produced some ace cricketers, who once played on the streets and in backyards and later performed on the world stage, bringing laurels to the country.

As we approached Uncle Mahfooz's house, we noticed the great excitement amongst the boys who were playing and the random crowd watching the game, as someone had just hit a 'Sixer'. This prompted all to scream and run in a state of unbounded excitement into the front yard and halfway onto the street.

Exotic flame trees lined this cul de sac. Its flamboyant display of orange flowers, was hugging the stone-faced bungalow. The entrance, adorned with delicate Jasmine creepers spreading their enchanting smell over the open verandah, led to a small quiet room.

Here, Mahfooz Uncle was resting on the bed, covered with clean, white cottons sheets, unaware of the youngsters' excitement outside.

He was all alone in the room. Only one thing gave him company; a once steaming cup of tea, complemented by a few broken pieces of everyone's favourite cumin biscuits, placed on a white quarter plate.

"There are few hours in life-more agreeable than the hour dedicated to the ceremony, known as afternoon tea."
- Henry James

As usual, Mahfooz Uncle's elaborate recliner, one of his few worldly possessions was next to his side table, with the daily newspaper and a pair of eyeglasses lying on it.

An old oleograph on the white washed walls distracted us. This probably must have been his favourite, for it had accompanied him here. I was once admiring it closely, when uncle explained in detail about its technique employed in it and the way it imitates oil painting. I was surprised to discover his keen interest in and knowledge of art. However, his deteriorating health had been taking a toll on all his interests.

We approached his room, and it was so quiet, that as soon as I opened the door, one could hear the squeaking of the hinges. Scared, that I might wake him up in case he was asleep, I crept on tiptoe silently into the room. The fluttering of the sheer cotton curtains, stirring gently in the breeze of the slow whirling ceiling fan nevertheless, appeared to be loud enough. The continuous ticking of the clock, ever so gently provided a sort of background sound which disturbed the quiet of this room.

It was so sad to see him in that state, all alone by himself.

Seeing us, he got up, slipped his thin feet with the veins clearly visible into his Mojari jodhpurs. Slowly balancing himself, he went outside to look for chairs for us to sit on. Seeing the garden chairs inside the small courtyard made him feel at ease.

The only thing that adorned this space were the jasmine bushes unfurling fragrance, while an aged Neem tree, compassionately spread its branches for the comfort of the pigeons as it provided shade all around, on that humid, sultry afternoon.

Strange as it may sound, no one seemed to be conscious of our presence. The aroma of fresh spices and fried onions drifted out of the kitchen door. A Siamese cat all curled up, contentedly purring away on one of the chairs with a distinct ambient but royal demeanour barely glancing at us. She had no choice but to jump off it, clearly not happy to relocate itself on the hard warm, cement floor which had the afternoon heat still trapped in it. The white pigeons perched up on the boundary wall, as if they just had a bath and were now basking in the sun to dry, left their feed for the moment and began to coo.

The whole ambiance was such that it evoked a feeling of tranquility in simplicity.

As we sat down, there was a pause! I glanced at Mahfooz uncle; He had tears blurring his eyes. I was perplexed, and could not wait to know why he was so sad!

Looking at me, he said, "I am feeling embarrassed to have you sit here, with the sun shining on a new bride's face and nothing to offer; as you are aware, I am living in someone else's house".

There was so much love in the way he said this. I stood up and kissed his forehead, saying that his love and presence were all that mattered.

On a later occasion, as we were leaving the country, I visited him again before our departure. That day he was quiet unwell. As I sat there at his bedside, I heard him say with a dazed expression, "I don't know when I will see you again, but there is a small piece of advice I would like to offer you.

"Simply love God and remember Him at all times to bring that 'Inner Light' into yourself."

I must have met him only a few times, but the message and wisdom he imparted became deeply ingrained in me for life. Although I did not pay too much attention to everything, he said at that time, his words have continued to echo in me since and until today. He sadly passed away a few months later. I miss him to this day and every day of my life.

Thirty years later - I once found myself sifting through the treasure trove of my husband's books in order to give away a few to a library. Books are greatly cherished in our family.

I was sitting on the hardwood floor with books piled all around me.

As I skimmed through their titles and contents, they brought back sweet memories and inspired deep thoughts. Some reminded of happier moments. A book with a green hardcover caught my attention. It was on 'Zikr' - Remembrance of God, and dedicated and autographed by none other than Uncle Mahooz himself. The title and the fact that he had signed it, made me jump a little and I was surprised at not having noticed this book earlier.

For the next few hours, I found myself rooted to the floor, reminiscing about the past as I browsed through the book. Strangely enough, he had highlighted all the important lines conveying deep and meaningful messages.

My experience with this elderly patriarch was the first instance that I had felt such a strong interest in spiritual teachings and a catalyst for reflection. I am almost certain that these encounters and experiences were meant to guide me at the time, I was ready to understand. As a wise man has said, the Master appears when the pupil is ready. It was many years later that this spiritual awakening was to take place in me.

Each time you meditate you create a stronger connection with
the world of Inner light, and happiness that exist within you."

Frederick Lenz

My work 'Tree of Life' paraphrases a couplet by
Bulleh Shah, the Mughal era Sufi poet and philosopher,
whose poetry focussed on the Oneness of the Creator.

# SUGAR TO SALT

"Life is 10% what happens to you
and 90% how you react to it."

Charles Swindoll

Mid 60's

I vividly recall my fascination, as a wonder-struck ten year old at the sight of these white mounds. With a beaming smile and sparkling eyes, inquisitive and excited, gazing with amazement at the mesmerizing sight of long, bamboo look-alike columnar stalks of sugar cane, entering the great industrial unit to be squeezed and crushed at one end; with mounds of snow-white tiny sugar crystals to appear magically at the other end.

Yahya uncle worked for the Jauharabad Sugar Mills. On his return from work, we all got ready to visit the Khewra Salt Mines. This ride would be the most delicious sweet and salty concoction, I would ever experience! It was nothing short of decadence personified; sugar in the morning and salt in the evening.

The landscape was spectacular; with hillocks, mountains, and barren gorges. Hidden among them were serene, picturesque fertile valleys, with clouds dancing over the nearby lakes. The happy moments, were the fights with my cousins over the peeled tangerines and apricots, until we arrived at the gates of the salt mines. With great excitement, we all boarded the train for a ride inside the mountain; to be remembered to this day.

This overwhelming experience of my first visit, which I vividly recall, was to propel me to make another trip to the salt mine years later. The whole scene flashed before my eyes.

This second visit in the 80's was moving and equally to be remembered. We and another couple bought the tickets to enter the salt Mine at the same time, and boarded the train for the same breathtaking tour.

The tour guide introduced himself saying, "I am a proud native of Khewra district, born, lived, and studied here. This amazing place is in close vicinity to the Jhelum River, and some 100 miles south of Pakistan's capital Islamabad."

He continued, "This salt range, which you are witnessing, is a subterranean mine and is said to be approximately 800 million years old. The geological shift over the years and the result of evaporation from the sea formed this range and covers the length of about 300 kilometers".

The simple young and energetic guide of ours was also to share an interesting story concerning this second largest salt mine of the world, as we entered the tunnel amidst the beauty of its dramatic natural salt formation which was to unfold in front of our eyes. Though overcome with an intense feeling of awe, I was fascinated beyond words. The term 'Rock and Roll' seemed to gel here, standing on the rock and revelling in the chill on the mountain, and rolling our tongues over the tangy sharp taste. I experienced all this in the cave, deep inside the mountain we were visiting.

With a microphone in his hand, amplifying the sound, the guide narrated, "It is believed that in 326 BC, Alexander the Great was making his way across the area that is now Pakistan. His army stopped for rest in this land. Somehow, here his horse began to lick the stones on the ground. Noticing that many other horses were also doing the same; a solider himself tried to lick one, and found that the rocks were quite salty. It was in this simple incident, the beautiful story emerged of the discovery of the Khewra Salt Mine."

What an amazing story this was! Its history made it even more interesting for us." Mining began during the Mughal period, before the Sikhs took over from them and later fell into the hands of the British somewhere around 1849". With this, the guide's tone and face changed; there was sadness in his voice as he narrated the scenes of oppression and the introduction of forced labour.

"The miners were not allowed to leave the mine till they had finished their assigned quota. This included pregnant women and children as well. It is thought that some were actually born inside the mine and later raised in orphanages, while a number had also died there upon birth." This was to explain the presence of the graves at the entrance of the mine which we were sad to see, and moreover upon knowing of the reason and the story behind them.

Mentioning this in a mellowed tone, he was to add, "I too was raised in an orphanage, in extremely deplorable conditions." He had gone quiet for a few seconds after saying this.

I saw the couple next to us in tears after hearing this from the guide. This story greatly moved the wife. With mixed feelings, we were walking along this amazing spectacle of nature, now with mixed feelings, witnessing the translucent colors, and rich hues of red, pink, and white inside the mountain.

Carrying a salty aroma, we approached the exit gates in awe of nature's splendor, while nurturing a friendship with our new acquaintances, which was to prove lasting. They were a perfect example of humility and a down to earth attitude.

We stopped at a Dhaba for a quick bite. This roadside restaurant was full of tourists, attracting every passerby, with the aroma that wafted so strongly from the kitchen, and the smoke that came out of its clay oven.

We had an enjoyable conversation, while having a simple but unbelievably tasty meal, of steaming roasted lamb with 'Naan', bread, hot and fresh, delicious until the last bite. The ever popular and famous bread was being prepared in front of us. It was fun to watch the thick dough, shaped into a ball and then like a circular disc, swirling and expanding in the air, then being thrown into the oven to bake, with a perfectly executed basketball shot.

This sumptuous meal left a taste after such a memorable day.

Since then, we kept in touch with our newfound friends.

A few years later at a charity event, I was delighted to see them sitting across the table.

We joined them. However, after a short while they excused themselves to leave. I asked them the reason for their desire to leave so early. With a short pause, she subtly mentioned, that she runs a girls orphanage, which she personally looks after. This raised mixed emotions in me; admiration, appreciation, and surprise.

She then went on to recount to me, how this thought of starting an orphanage had come into her mind; after their visit at the Khewra Salt Mines, when the tour guide had mentioned the story of the orphans and himself being raised at an orphanage.

It was this empathic idea, which had motivated them into to start one. They had felt that their large ancestral home, which was lying empty and unoccupied, was perfect for housing an orphanage.

A few days later, she invited me to visit this place.

Upon arrival, a female superintendent welcomed me graciously. It was heartwarming to see such a serene and nurturing environment It being a lovely summer evening, it made some girls enjoy sitting in the well-manicured garden, watching and cheering for their friends playing badminton. This once being my favourite sport, I too felt an urge to join them on the court.

Seeing us enter, the girls immediately came to receive and greet us. My friend introduced me to them in the manner as a mother would.

As the brightness of the sun began to fade away, the girls came in for the evening prayers and the approaching dinnertime. All were so happy to see us join them on the big dining table. We had a quick bite to make them happy. When we got up, they all stood up as well in respect and asked us to sit with them a little longer. One just so sweetly came to ask, "Aunty, you haven't eaten much, can I make some tea for you?" This gesture by this girl took our heart away forever. The family strives to make them live a normal life, going to schools and colleges to pursue their studies, and learn the dying art of managing a home. It was as if they were coming out from a finishing school.

They all looked like one big family. Surely, this will be the place, they will always remember as their home - surrounded by friends and cared by a generous affectionate mother; who will live in their hearts and who they will cherish forever.

Walking around with her, I thought to myself, what amazing humanitarian work she is doing, and with such dedication. But "What if she did not have the financial resources to sustain a project like this"? Could it be that only a selected few have a love to serve humanity?

We were moving through the corridor, with these questions in my mind, when I was introduced to the supervisor who seemed to share the same sense of devotion and commitment as my friend, and a heart full of compassion, but unlike her without the requisite resources.

This was, as if I received a direct answer to my, question!

The supervisor was a key member of the project, looking after the center, also acting as a conduit, to the outside world, introducing people to this institution.

It was truly edifying to see how one person so seamlessly interwoven with this family for a noble common cause.

As I left, wishing them the best, I felt completely overwhelmed by their dedication, as well as the time and resources for the good of the humanity at large.

It was raining on the way out. Quickly I folded my umbrella as I sat in the car. A loud honking of the horn from a van behind me disturbed my reverie. Some people are so impatient.

On the way while driving, my thoughts travelled back in time, triggering the memory of a classmate of mine, who was my childhood friend. Rukhsana lived close by, and our whole family loved her.

We were coming home early, as it was a half-day at school. Rukhsana asked if I could come over to help her with the luncheon preparation, as they are expecting some guests.

I agreed, and quickly left my heavy school bag at home, as I yelled from the door to my mother, "Ammi, I will be back soon" - Needless to say I later got punished from my mom, for not taking her prior permission, and rightly so, for I was brought up in a very disciplined manner.

Entering Rukhsana's house, I was surprised to see the elaborate setting of the table with formal dinner service, cutlery, and an abundance of sumptuous gourmet food. My surprise was greater when I learnt that, the guests were young innocent children from the orphanage.

Every year, this family would invite them to have lunch, and spend the day at their place. To these children, this was a great occasion and adventure, as seldom did they get the chance to go out. They cherish to enter a new world; even for a day.

The children and Rukhsana's family all mingled and spent quality time together. I remember the delight on their young faces and their innocent expressions when they arrived, and later, when food was served for them at the table. Some in sheer excitement, some children just grabbed what was in front of them, while others well behaved, and still some, shy and polite, waited for them to be served. After they had finished eating and polished off their plates, the look of satisfaction on their faces was almost beyond words.

Rukhsana and her mother, had also prepared the gifts, wrapped beautifully, for each one of their little guests in order to give them a warm send off.

On the way back, to drop them off, we stopped by our house to get permission from my mother to accompany them for the ice cream treat, as I was left with no chance of making a second mistake.

The children were unaware of this surprise; a treat that anyone would simply love any time of the day. Enjoying which, even a seventy year old, could be like a seven-year-old child. The scene of seeing them entering the ice cream parlour that afternoon has always remained.

In sheer delight, they had jumped in excitement, seeing the myriad rainbow of flavours. Twisting their heads sideways, like birds looking at a tasty morsel and rolled their tongues over the melting ice cream - torn between finishing it quickly and wishing at the same time that it would never finish! Some desired more and did not want to leave, savouring this cold delicious concoction.

It was overwhelming to see these children, deprived even of these simple, small pleasures. Thinking about it makes me sad even now.

I was reminded, as I am now of the several occasions, when my parents would mention going out for ice cream, and how that offer motivated me to finish my homework quickly, as seldom before.

While helping them clean up after the children were dropped back safely, I realized that it was Rukhsana's birthday, but this gracious family, celebrated it in such a compassionate noble way.

That experience of seeing their emotional involvement in those young lives in that manner was deeply moving for me, to say the least.

They had been performing this noble task for years, without anyone knowing of their compassion. Their faces reflected the beauty in their hearts.

Spending the evening with them, I was to realize that beyond our pre-conceived, basic physical needs, there are powerful deep-rooted emotional needs as well, which need to be satisfied and they constantly beautify and nourish the entire being.

With such display of love, they were supporting and encouraging these young children to become positive and productive, while developing empathy, towards other individuals, and growing up to lead their life with confidence and dignity.

Such experiences with friends had a strong effect on changing my perspective, in leading our lives.

The Dalai Llama has put this so aptly:

> "God human qualities, honesty, sincerity, good heart cannot be bought by money, nor can they be produced by machines; but only by the mind itself; we can call this the inner light or God's blessings or human qualities. This is the essence of mankind."

To paraphrase this, I would say, God's Attributes, which are the embodiment of 'Inner light'.

# ON THE INCENSE TRAIL

Saudi Arabia 80's-90's

I was starting my new life in Riyadh, almost in the middle of the Arabian Peninsula; the largest Peninsula in the world. The southern part lay along the route of the caravans that had plied between the Indian Sub-continent and the Middle East to Europe from the 7th century onward; transporting goods and fuelling trade. Different cultures and languages had inter-mingled, bringing uniqueness to a land, which is a cradle of Islamic civilization. This route had become an established artery - the famous incense and silk trade route.

During school days, I had made an embroidered artwork of a caravan scene, as travel stories always fascinated me. My father had gone around scavenging and looking for appropriate material, which I could incorporate in this work of mine. Little did I know then, that I would become a part of that landscape by living in a country, which was an important part of the route taken by such caravans. This work later won a regional award at an exhibition held by (RCD) Regional Cooperation for Development between three nations, Pakistan, Iran, and Turkey.

**My embroidered winning entry at the exhibition**

The peninsula has vastly unpopulated spaces; among which is the Rub-al Khali; also known as the Empty Quarter, the largest contiguous sand desert. The area is largely unexplored and uninhabited, being the earth's hottest and driest place with sandy arid wilderness. A few Bedouin tribes brave this place and are still, settled around the edges.

To some extent, I experienced the wilderness, harshness and challenging environment of the Bedouin existence on a trip into the desert, and with it saw a woman's compassion and her deep faith in our Creator.

While teaching, on one of our school trips, I witnessed the unpredictability and speed at which the running sands could move.

It was a lovely spring day. Our vibrant, energetic, young principal, I and four other teachers accompanied the fourth graders; all lovely sweet girls, towards the escarpment driving past a scene of raw beauty with the sedimentary layers of rock formations along the way. The girls were singing, wind blowing through the bus and over our faces. We were all in a jovial mood, looking forward to an enjoyable day's excursion.

On our way, the principal decided to stop at the sand dunes as the weather was just perfect, with a light breeze.

This area was in true sense an empty quarter with undulations of shades of beige, changing its colour every now and then, which naturally team with the winds direction, and its strength clearly displaying the low and high linear mounds, creating impressive dune formations.

This trip was going to be an experience of a lifetime.

All of us were responsible for the five girls. The climb was not easy on these mounds. It was unmarked and without any path. With every step, our legs would sink half a foot into the moving sand, and we had to make great effort to lift our feet out of the surging sand to take another step. Since none of us was used to this measure of walking on loose sand, our leg muscles were ready to give up with the rigorous workout.

The girls however were thoroughly enjoying themselves, running all over the place, jumping and sliding over these sand ridges, while the sand itself was moving and travelling.

From gradual to sudden, the wind picked up and started blowing hard; I witnessed right in front of my eyes the shifting of the sand, moving from one mound to the other. This was an indescribable and overwhelming, scary sight and an uncontrollable situation for us. If one mound would sink, the other would rise.

I myself was screaming and trying to bring the girls together and hold each other's hands, but with the strong presence of the whistling wind, I could not even hear my own voice as it disappeared into the unknown. At this moment, we counted the children, to find one girl missing. We found ourselves losing track of each other, with the added responsibility of the girls looming over our heads.

Following our sixth sense blindly, we tried to reach a point from where the road would be visible. With God's grace, we noticed we were heading in the right direction. However, we discovered that two were still missing. Low visibility and the whirling sand, was adding to our difficulties in the search. The second missing person was the teacher, whom we finally saw waving at us with her orange scarf, her legs half-submerged in the sand dunes, and we noticed that she was trying to keep her balance, and profusely trying to pull the little girl, who had been lost to us out of the sand.

Luckily, with all the strength she could muster, she was able to pull out the girl. This holding the girl in her arms, this brave woman waved at us. Her emotions were obvious. We all clapped and cheered heartily and breathed a sigh of relief.

It was difficult to find our way back, though we were not far from where we had started. However, I remembered the ostrich egg shells that were scattered all over the place which were to assist us finding a path to the place from where we had started.

Such was the howling of the wind, that we could not hear one another. Our eyes, ears, and nose; all filled with sand. I am sure that the desert sand must still be residing in me, making a little dune somewhere even now.

Only God had saved us on that occasion and after we all got back safe, we were to thank Him most sincerely and profoundly for this miracle.

When we sat in the bus, we asked our colleague, "What went through your mind while rescuing the girl from the sand and putting your own life in danger, knowing that you have the responsibility of your own daughter and a husband back home"?

She was to reply with confidence, that "My entire being simply wanted to rescue this girl, and I can only thank God for helping me to succeed in this ordeal. Nothing else mattered at that moment."

This little girl got a second lease on life through the woman's compassion and her deep belief in God.

I too lived that moment experiencing the omnipotent power of the Creator.

The senses could not fully fathom this powerful and strange phenomenon. Every second, the staggering landscape was different. An incident like this proved that our human existence is just a mere speck in the vastness of the universe.

After settling down, to explore Riyadh, we again drove further towards the escarpment, viewing the vast expanses of a different terrain again without greenery. The spectacular vertical cliffs held their presence, with a breathtaking view at the sight of the steep, 'Edge of the world'. There is a sharp drop, with a splendid view of the dry rocky plains below.

We stood there and saw this from afar, as the high temperatures, prevented us from getting closer and availing this on the hike, and sadly postponed until later. Surprised to see an old man, sitting in the shadow of the rock, with bottles of water, stacked in a bag next to him. I noticed that without taking any money; he gave the bottle to a couple, who had started braving up the incline.

I was deeply touched as always, at seeing good deeds in the most unexpected of places.

This was an unforgettable drive and to a place, where the sunrise and sunsets dominate the whole horizon, boldly emerging and receding, and nothing to stop them, through the thorny acacia trees.

It was not just geographically that it was so different, but new in many ways, from the country in which I had grown up. It exposed me to a new culture, people, language and climate; all of which I was now experiencing for the first time; and later I not only became acclimatised, but was fortunate enough to have many exciting and happy experiences.

This was the era of the eighties, a period during which and the following decade Saudi Arabia was to enter an era of rapid growth, development and prosperity, driven by the gushing wells of black gold - Oil, which became the Kingdom's main economic lifeline.

The most precious, ever-lasting memory for me of those years of my life is that our three sons, Samir, Asim and Omar were born here. They are certainly my great joy and my driving force. Raising them and taking care of the family has been a privilege and one of the highlights of my life's journey.

Interesting memories are still etched in my mind to this day; of landing on this new soil. A mere few fleeting glances at what beheld at the Riyadh airport, gave me a half-lucid view of a country, I would now be living in for an unforeseeable time to come.

A short stocky uniformed man with a forced half smile and pleasantness stood there receiving passengers at the arrival gate. I heard him say, 'Ahlan wa Sehlan', a couple of times, and another 'Kaif ul haal'. The flat tones implied that the greetings were formal at best. Every now and then, during this short time, another term that was to register itself instantly with me, was "Ma'alish". Of course I was to understand only later what they meant. Faced with this, distinct meaningful element of speech repeated so frequently, my fellow passengers and I started mimicking the words and learnt the few Arabic phrases immediately. I sensed that these few words uttered unfeelingly, had made me an instant Arabic expert.

The phrases that I used confidently were later to help me in connecting at that time with other citizens.

Soon enough, I was to discover that in this land we would usually be greeted with a distinct warm welcome; whose warmth appeared to compete with its high temperatures outside, and hot enough to keep the food warm and dry the clothes almost instantly. I found out and was almost certain, by the time, I would hang the next batch of washed laundry, the earlier batch would almost be dry! An added bonus for going through this ordeal was that I would be getting a free sauna treatment, every time stepping into the open, for any length of time. However, the presence of the dryer, later made me count my blessings.

Those days, not many women were out in the open. Few that were there, exuded an Arabian aura, in a black silk cloak, the 'Abaya' flowing over them.

Later, I too wore the Abaya, when going out, which transported me to the mystique world they lived in. I felt like a princess, enjoying this embellished, flowy dress. I realized that it suited their harsh desert climate, and at the same time maintained their modesty. The whole scene presented an aura of femininity, blending their culture and values, with the cosmopolitan society. It was interesting to see this distinct dress statement: Men in white and women in black.

Once on a blazing hot day, the temperature searing to a high 40 degrees Celsius, which is normal there during the summer months with life going on as usual. The desert heat did not prevent me and other women from venturing into the traditional markets - the 'Souks' that were soaked in the exotic smells of spices, coffee and frankincense; and lined with jewellery shops with amazing displays, most unusually; hanging from the ceiling down to the floor. Yes, that is true: Seeing was believing!

**My fascination with Bedoiun jewellery, made me engrave them on pewter**

I was always perplexed by the thought of what would happen to all the gold and valuables seen in these shops, when most of them leave their businesses and go to the mosque. The shopkeepers simply covered the enticing and dazzling gold jewelry with a mere light curtain, and leave to offer their prayers in congregation, with utmost faith that nobody would touch a thing in their shops while they were away. This was the level of trust and honesty prevalent at that time. In today's world, one cannot imagine that this would even be possible.

The traits of warmth and hospitality embedded so deep in the tradition, simply overwhelmed me. It would be very rare to encounter their likes elsewhere.

We gradually settled down in a completely new environment and in our new home.

As soon as we moved into our lovely new neighbourhood, we received as a welcoming gesture from our wonderful neighbours an elaborate Arabic food platter. That simple gesture made an instant connection with them and provided us with an instant sense of belonging. It actually made us feel comfortable, and a part of their family.

Getting to know the Syed family was a blessing. They had a well-established business in Riyadh and olive groves in Jordan.

Whenever they received the fresh produce, from their groves, they sent it to us as well. My taste buds soon fell in love with this delight and a chance to savour, the best olives and the first cold press of the extra virgin oil. I enjoyed this treat throughout our stay in Riyadh.

I visited this family often, and every time, I would be lovingly served with two or three servings of high tea. The first one would be as soon as I arrived; the second serving was complemented with dates; and the third offered with homemade 'Ma'amoul', the famous date biscuits of the Arab world. Soon, I found myself actually waiting anxiously for the third round, as these biscuits were simply delicious. If the opportunity had presented itself, I would have finished off all of them.

Though I really enjoyed the Ma'amouls, I was confused by the name of these biscuits, conditioned as I was by the term in my native language, Urdu, to think and relate that word to 'Routine'. However in Arabic, the word means, 'To do'.

All these gestures had certainly assisted in creating an instant bond, and the friendship blossomed after the ritual of these three cups of tea. During one of my initial visits, my experience of having tea at their place was delightfully funny. After finishing my tea, I placed the cup with the right side up, as one would normally do, but I was surprised that someone promptly refilled the cup. This sequence was to continue for the second, and again the third time. This intrigued me. Little did I know then that if one does not want any more, the cup should tip over and wave it gently a couple of times, to signal to the tea pourer, that you want no more.

The simple ignorance of their normal etiquette must have given them the impression that I was an over the top tea junkie.

Imtiaz, with whom I had developed an instant bond, was the beautiful and gracious woman of this house. A woman with a charitable, compassionate heart, she had been volunteering and helping the families of patients at the hospitals, and was a working mother, an administrator at the Arabic school. Their eldest daughter Sausun, instantly became my friend. She was our interpreter and the sole link between Imtiaz and me. Both of us were confident in our conversation, she in Arabic and me in English.

Imtiaz, like many others later, were to become a conduit in instilling and in making me contribute some good in that new environment. Our extraordinary relationship between us continues to this day. They would never let us go, without having dinner. We would be so satiated that you wished for a pillow to snooze. Though this gesture is noticeable in every Saudi household, it is also seen in most cultures irrespective of their status.

Growing up I had always seen similar thoughtfulness, towards our families and our then neighbours at the time, but these gestures only touched me, when someone else did them so genuinely for me.

In those days, the environment too was certainly unconventional and unique. The Hejazi architecture certainly fascinated me and my interest made me observe everything closely amongst others. It was very different from what I was used to and incorporated a feature of carved wooden screens on projecting windows popularly known as 'Mashrebiyah', which was esthetically pleasing and was intended for privacy.

When living in Jeddah, we often visited the old quarter of Al Balad and we would walk pass through some ancestral family homes having this feature, that still exist in Jeddah's old by lanes and narrow alleys, where a distinct sense of nostalgia prevails.

**Mashrebiyah in the old Quarter of Jeddah**

While noticing these Mashrebiyah's, I thought to myself that this was in a way a unique one-way mirror. What a cleverly devised way it was, of having the residents enjoy their cherished privacy, with a good view of the outside, without being visible.

I was lucky to be behind such a screen once, albeit for a while, almost - a sneak preview! Yes, I availed this simple pleasure of seeing the world go by, and the reality that surrounds the residents in the closed quarters of this house. This was as I sipped the deliciously refreshing, hot aromatic coffee in a handle-less cup, 'Estikan', served elegantly from a lovely, typically Middle Eastern coffee pot.

My few minutes behind this, 'One way mirror' made me see this moving scene, from within my comfort zone.

This house fronted a main thoroughfare, though not a busy street. A few cars passed by fleetingly to distract us, every now and then in the opposite by-lane.

Curious to see through the Mashrebiyah from inside, and without giving much importance, I caught one view that was to catch my attention was of skinny young children running around their mother's bare feet; seeming to be quite vulnerable, yet not bothered by the heat in those summer months, sitting on the hot paved sidewalk, without any shade.

The excitement to enjoy the view and experience was to fade, as I noticed this from the comfort of an elegant air-conditioned room.

With a half-filled Estikan, still in my hand, I saw a car slowly appear and then stop. A woman fully covered in her Abaya, gently stepped out, holding two bags, and approached these women. The children and the women ran towards the bags, almost trying to be the first to grab them and ready to snatch from each other. The donated clothes thrown all over the pavement were quickly to be picked up in a tug-of-war, by whoever got the chance to reach them first.

Meanwhile, a young ten or twelve year old boy, also stepped out of the car, holding a peeled tangerine. He was just about to put one wedge in his mouth, when he saw the looks of anticipation on the children present. He immediately gave a wedge each to these children and quickly took out another one from his lunch box and gave them that too.

It seemed that this woman and the young boy could not bear their desperation and instantly took out their grocery bags from the car, and gave them those as well.

I simply forgot all about my tea, seeing this unforgettable sight of anguish and frustration. I stood up and left with a heavy heart, remembering the vulnerability of all those affected and the compassion of the other. Though difficult to fathom, the disparity did exist side by side. Those moving moments seen through the beautiful intricate Mashrebiyah which I had admired, were to make me realize my own due role in this regard, of reaching out.

While appreciating these beautiful screens, I would often wish that they were in my house too. For at times, I with my young children stepped out onto the balcony of our house to have a two-in-one pleasure of getting some fresh, even if warm air, and a glimpse of the world outside. As I noticed the passerby bemused, it would dawn on me that it was unusual then in Saudi society, to see a young twenty five year old standing in an open balcony without an Abaya.

However, when this became apparent, I never did so again.

It is very interesting to observe that modern constructions even now, incorporate this unique architectural feature; though it is one of the few distinct characteristics from the past, which they proudly and aptly preserved and introduced in the present. Like in any other place, with new generations, fresh ideas and trends have naturally followed; making this place an urban metropolitan city. This in hindsight, overshadowed the glorious past in aspects.

This was a truly multicultural society and something of a melting pot, as all cultures mingled and blended well here with their different traditions and identities, different, yet at the core all very similar. This was also to provide an opportunity to make some everlasting friendships.

**Multiculturalism and One World**

**Identity**

What touched me most and stood out significantly, was the compassionate nature and generosity of the inhabitants of this land; and which I had the good fortune to experience during my stay there.

I soon became accustomed and felt fully adjusted to this new environment; following which I had started enjoying my existence in this country and so much so, that I was quite unhappy at leaving it.

This country, certainly seem to grow on one, and for me it will always remain special as it must, to many others, who have lived there. I still feel after all these years, that a part of me continues to live there.

# ONE ON ONE WITH ROYALTY

Riyadh 2005

Once, heading for the interview, I was to find myself caught up in the early morning rush hour. Interestingly this is a daily joyride and a common denominator we share in all major cities. The driving skills are tested at every moment, as each driver attempts to gain those precious few minutes by over taking others, charged with a rush of adrenalin, blood pressure rising.

Even if uninterested, one cannot but notice the shiny brand new luxury cars, while some still chugging along in their old ones, the motor bikes zooming through, like gusts of wind through a tunnel, taking advantage of the situation by following their own rules and in full control of their destinies.

This was quite an experience, yet certainly not a joy ride.

With my blood pressure under control, I managed to reach the American school campus, almost in time. The parking lot inside the school area was about 500 metres away from the main building. I made my way past the barbed barriers placed for security reasons. The clearance from the check post was essential.

Three guards looked at me from top to bottom, as if scanning me like an X-ray machine. I had to go through this scrutiny from them to be able to meet my 10 o'clock appointment as scheduled.

I was dressed appropriately with stilettos, which I felt would be both, formal and comfortable. Well! Not as I had thought. The walk, on a cemented sidewalk was long. The best thing I could have done was to take off my shoes and carry them. My feet would certainly have thanked me for this thoughtful gesture.

Upon my arrival at the administration office, the secretary at the reception desk gave me a multi page form to fill, as if I was applying for an MBA program; and which I swiftly completed. She then escorted me to the Principal's office.

The Principal instantly made me feel comfortable. We started off with such a lovely casual conversation in a manner, that I did not realize that this was actually my interview for a job.

After cursorily examining my portfolio, she asked me to substitute for a month, as an Art teacher for grade twelve students. I felt this at the time to be a tough call! Dabbling in art is one thing but teaching art is altogether a different ball game. However challenges make us rise to the occasion from time to time.

I enjoyed this short teaching assignment. It was an exciting and refreshing experience, akin to the feelings of a child upon entering an ice cream shop. What a better way than to be with children, recharging one's own batteries whilst transferring creative, artistic thoughts to them at the same time.

As I nearly settled, and started to enjoy teaching; when I was lucky again to receive another exciting offer, just a few days later.

It must have been 3 o'clock when the final bell rang. There was hustle and bustle all around, with the teachers and children, all packing in a rush to go home, and as was I.

I was surprised to see the Principal's secretary standing outside the class wanting to talk to me. She came inside and said, "The Principal wants to see you for a minute." A bit perturbed, I headed with her to the Principal's office. After the usual niceties, she casually asked, "The King's niece is looking for a private art tutor for her daughter - Would I be interested? Perplexed, and unsure about what she had just said, I requested her to repeat again. Yes, I heard it right; it was actually the King's niece.

She asked me that if I was interested, to contact her as soon as possible.

This was exciting! In anticipation, I called the princess the next evening. She too seemed enthusiastic and graciously talked to me in English- albeit with a pronounced Arabic accent.

The elegant and graceful Princess Mounira Al Sudairi invited me to what was to prove to be a pleasant dinner. I was happy beyond words and found out that this was not unusual in their culture, and this was a deep-rooted Arabian custom and an integral part of their life.

This was truly special for me - going to a palace with an invitation from a princess.

The guards at the palace gates were duly briefed about my expected arrival. They escorted me along the grand drive, surrounded by beautiful manicured gardens with desert perennials.

Tall stately palm trees appeared to be standing like guards, holding verdant umbrellas in the 40 degree Celsius heat, desperately trying to give shade along the driveway, leading to the palace entrance - Wow! Seemed as if I was in a big Spanish resort.

The Princess in a long pink floral dress with a chiffon scarf, gracefully covering her hair, came to receive me very graciously. She gave me a hug and holding my hand with a big welcoming smile and in a gentle soft voice, she said 'Ahlan wa Sehlan'. This was a greeting I had heard many a time and every time I had felt truly honoured.

Her beautiful persona reflected a sense of style and cultural milieu, exuding class, and the true elegance of a princess, conveying a certain presence and sophistication beyond words. This was evident in the interior of her palace; statement furniture pieces and beautiful artwork adorned the walls. The white marble floor sparkled with Persian rugs floating on them.

One work of art that caught my eye was by the famous Pakistani artist Gulgee's in Lapis Lazuli. This celestial blue semi-precious stone is also a symbol of royalty.

Royals and connoisseurs the world over appreciated and cherished his work, adding it to their collections.

**With Gulgee, at his home in the early 90's.**

The entire decor, steeped in Islamic culture, was understated opulence. I felt it was the hallmark of her personal style and taste. We enjoyed a very casual friendly conversation. She was so down to earth, that I could not believe that I was meeting this genuine beautiful princess for the first time. Immediately I was served with drinks and dates; probably the best I've ever eaten.

I was later introduced to the members of Princess Mounira's family, including the matriarch, her mother and elders who made me feel like their own daughter; all dignified and stately, yet unpretentious; seated gracefully on the elaborately set dining table. Gourmet food was served in gold-rimmed dinnerware embossed with the coat of arms that matched perfectly with similar insignia on the flatware and crystal, complemented with the view of the outside lawn.

In all innocence, I asked her about the relationships between her and the other members of the family; as they were being so respectfully attended to, only to be embarrassed to find out that they were the ruling King Fahd's sisters!

All of those present were close family members of the royal family, and they made me feel comfortable as if I was one of them, showing love and importance. For me, this was love at first sight with these royals.

The close family had gathered that day, as the King was unwell.

Throughout the dinner, the Princess herself, placed food gently on our plates, in a marked gesture of respect for her elders and me too, as a guest.

It was approaching the evening prayer time. We all got up, the maids joining as well, and we all prayed together.

Then, what was to leave a lasting impression on me was that as soon as we had finished dinner, the maids who were serving everyone, were offered the very same delicacies we had enjoyed on that elaborately laid table.

This scene was to remind me of a couplet in Urdu by Iqbal; the famous poet and philosopher, in eulogizing the act of standing together in answer to the prayer call. The Mahmood referred to in this instance, is the Sultan Mahmood of Ghazna, whose devoted slave was Ayaz.

Aik hee saf main kharay ho gayay Mahmood o Ayaz Na koee banda raha na banda nawaz

Mahmood (The Sultan) and Ayaz (The slave) in a single file stood side by side,
Their remained no servant nor master, nothing did them divide.

Even in such a royal household, there was no distinction between rich and poor. Their genuine graciousness, hospitality, and humility were beyond words - certainly a very eye opening experience for me, of the true values and practices of nobility.

On the day the King passed away, I visited my friend to offer my condolences. The fifth Monarch of Saudi Arabia, King Fahd passed away on 1st August 2005 after his 23-year rule. The family was in mourning, all in black Abayas praying silently. I too joined them.

Over the years, our friendship was to thrive and the Princess became one of my treasured friends.

# A DAY OUT

The more I traveled; the more I saw that people everywhere are similar despite their different religious or cultural backgrounds. Their need to care for each other, give back to their communities, take care of loved ones, and the need to be loved, transcends cultural and geographical boundaries. I noticed such incidences in two different parts of the world that made me feel that people are inherently kind and compassionate, no matter where they are or where they come from.

One such experience was during my stay in Saudi Arabia. The Arabian climate, ever so pervasive, plays a major role, in dictating our mood. The warm sultry months makes one want to jump into the water. However, I must confess that I did not know how to swim then; neither do I today. Otherwise, being in a pool, day in and day out would be everybody's dream.

The idea of outdoor activity was farfetched. To give oneself a treat, the bookstore was an ideal option to browse the books. Interestingly; as expected, most of the shelves displayed Arabic books. The few in English that were available were not the books, one that would have interested me.

However there was one advantage in our frequent visits to the bookstore, the books, we had picked up to browse on our last visit, would still be there on the shelf, and we could pick up and continue reading where we had left off the last time and eventually complete them, without the onus of having to buy them.

This became our favourite ritual. One evening, we went to the bookstore and were disappointed to find it closed for prayers. Unfortunately we were just a few minutes late.

It was captivating to hear the muezzin's call to prayer from a beautifully designed small hypostyle mosque. This courtyard design inspired by the Prophet's Mosque in Medina, is favoured all over. This call to prayer coming simultaneously from various nearby mosques would almost sound like a cacophony. Upon hearing it, there would be the spontaneous, almost synchronised act of closing down all business activity temporarily. A ripple effect followed and everything soon closed. People, young and old, came from different directions, to make their way to the mosque. Even their wait at the pedestrian crossing seemed to be too long for them.

Instead of waiting for the bookstore to open, we decided to drive a little further outwards to the periphery of Riyadh city. This road was dotted with Istaraha's. The closest definition of the term would be a wayside tea or coffee house to break your journey, rest and enjoy.

Our few minutes stop at an Isteraha, even if brief in order to get directions at this men only domain, allowed us to delve into their evenings, and gave us a chance to listen to 'Nabati' poetry, which is unique to the Arabian Peninsula. This was quite an unexpected experience and setting, to witness a classic literary tradition and listen to this ancient form of poetry. I only wished I knew the language, so that I could really understand what he was reciting; as it is never the same, when someone translates it for you.

A waiter noticing that we were still there brought hot Kahwa (coffee) for us as well. Thoroughly enjoying and cheerfully repeating the recital in a half-melodious voice, this jolly old fellow was serving hot Kahwa to the people sitting in the open air, lazily perched on benches, almost appearing ready to sleep.

There is a Bedouin proverb,

"When you sleep in a house, your thoughts
are as high as the ceiling, when you sleep
outside, they are as high as the stars."

The ambiance of such evenings brightens their life till late into the night, as it would be in most places, but more so in this country because of the weather. The warm breeze, which by definition is still a breeze, lifts one's spirits. The people and even the cats all come out of hibernation. These stray cats are awake because of the general noisy activity in these late hours.

This was like a 'Midsummer's night dream', on a stark dark night. We were now heading home after a very enjoyable evening.

As we drove steadily past the intersection, into the right lane, passing by a large vacant plot, towards our compound. I suddenly noticed, a Clowder of cats coming from nowhere in this darkness and gathering in one place, as if to attend some pre-arranged cats' convention. Being a family of cat lovers, we decided to stop to see what was going on! Another car stopped behind us as well, possibly to see this unusual sight.

To our surprise, we saw an elderly man step out of the car, open the trunk, take out a big tray and advance towards the cats. He was carrying the tray carefully and reverently, as if handling a treasure. These famished felines ran towards the man and meeting him halfway, jumped on the food impatiently, bought with so much love and affection. One could hear them purr-ing away in contentment after a real feast. It was a moving sight and experience and a delight to hear them purring away.

To enjoy and view the scene better, for it was dark we stepped out of the car and kept watching in amazement, at the sight of these grey, white, and black felines, in all sizes, small and not so small, their eyes shining like a 5-watt night light in the dark.

Speaking to him, greater was our surprise, when we were told, he comes here every day on his return from work. He would go home, pick up the food tray his wife had prepared, and bring it here for the cats. It was truly amazing and awe-inspiring for us to hear his ethical and a 'purr-fect' moral obligation that he had undertaken.

This elderly man, probably of Turkish descent, had taken this responsibility of feeding the unattended felines for many years, while enjoying their presence around him each night.

Observing our amazement, he promptly shared a little story with us of the days gone by.

"During the Ottoman rule, the state had advised the butchers to go on a break, after every few months, because they thought that slaughtering animals and cutting their meat every day, might destroy their emotions and feelings of mercy. In their free period, they were asked to involve themselves in gardening and taking care of the plants, in order for them to retain and regain their feelings of compassion."

He was to add, "Sharing these stories helps one another in performing similar gestures."

While going back to his car, in a sad tone, he remarked, "Sometimes it's worrisome when a few cats are missing, as I now recognize most of them".

This late night trip was engaging and touching! It made me reflect on how beautifully this universe works. Each one of us has been assigned certain duties to perform and avail opportunities that may come our way.

We arrived at home ready to enjoy our coffee, still thinking about this inspiring man.

I had a similar exciting encounter in Turkey. During our few days stay, I noticed their love for cats, 'Kedi' in Turkish. For some, they are part of their lives.

While in Istanbul, we spent a very pleasant morning, visiting the 6th century Byzantine monument the Hagia Sophia. This was once a church, later a mosque, and now a museum. Walking past the eternal resting places of the Ottoman royals, we went across just a few metres to appreciate and view the grandeur of the Blue mosque with its tall impressive six minarets and a chance to say our afternoon prayers. This was the first imperial mosque, where the powerful king, Sultan Ahmed 1 lies quietly outside its precincts. Our plan was to spend the afternoon inside the oldest traditional covered market. Meandering through the bustling back streets and its by lanes, through the Sahaflar Carsisi (Book Bazaar), not ignoring the tombs of the known and many unknown, their forgotten past seemed to gel with the living world. In the narrow pathways, cats availing their right of way, moved shyly with the passerbys. Few curled on windowsills in a daze with the strong Sheesha fumes, that had permeated the cafes, and lively restaurants serving food on the outside tables unaware, of someone's resting place just across, separating them only by a stone fence. Even with so many exhilarating sites, one could not ignore the presence of cats in this exotic city of historical gems, snoozing and curling in the mosque courtyards confidently purring away, ignorant of sleeping next to a age old sarcophagus.

After a lovely day roaming around - an enchanting time in itself, I experienced an eclectic mix of the mundane, worldly and the spiritually uplifting and thought provoking sights. With these mixed feelings, we entered the covered walkway, passing through a labyrinth of side streets. I could not help, but noticed that an adorable white Angora cat was following us around, in this city's admired centuries old Grand bazaar. This beautiful breed has its origins in the Ankara region of Turkey.

I just could not resist her charm and beauty and promptly decided to take her home.

It was indeed surprising to see this domesticated breed in such a crowded atmosphere with no less than four thousand shops, which attracted thousands of visitors each day.

A shopkeeper bemused at seeing this pleasant sight said something in Turkish. I stopped and tried to understand, what he was trying to communicate to me, from behind the mounds of multicoloured aromatic spices he was offering. His display of mouth watering dry fruits and spices, were a visual delight, in this covered bazaar.

Noticing my blank expression, a young boy from this shop, frustratingly shrugging his shoulders, went running in a lane nearby, and returned at what appeared to be, the speed of light.

With a beaming smile on his youthful face, he opened a small jar, with contained food for Kedi; whilst repeating in a joyful tone, the words 'Kedi et, kedi et'; or Meat for cats.

Upon seeing the jar, the blue-eyed white Angora leapt towards me circling around and purring away in joy. I stooped to gently pet and gave her tiny piece. She quickly gulped it down, the movement clearly visible moving sideways and down, despite the thick white hair. Without wasting time, I found her desperately waiting for the second round.

After having had her fill, she seemed to have given up her inclination to follow me around, perhaps preferring to retire for a little snooze. Though I was sure that sometimes later, she would undoubtedly repeat this gesture with another passerby.

Such acts and display of love and compassion must have been present, in these centuries old civilization times and time again. Their incredible compassionate nature allows them, even to let the street dogs enter the malls, during those harsh winter months.

Certainly this exotic city of Istanbul would appear to have a love affair with cats. It is often said there that, "Without a cat, Istanbul would lose its soul."

In street bazaars and roadside restaurants, these cuddly, timid felines move around confidently, among passersby; to be loved and be fed. They even seem to own the restaurant owners as well and often find a safe niche, to stretch and curl comfortably. For these smart Kedilar's, the 'Do not disturb' sign is not an essential requirement for them when resting, for their alarm system is very powerful and is 'on the alert' all the time throughout their life.

The Ottoman Imperial family loved these felines as much as the Egyptians and Arabs, and perhaps in their own way, their favourite felines have lived and seen the rise and fall of empires.

I am almost convinced that this lovable, cuddly race of carnivorous mammal has the ability to bring love and compassion on themselves, from people around them.

I kept thinking about these incidences and the more I thought, the more I realize that the rush of the people to the mosque, in response to the call for prayer, and that of the cats towards their food were very similar in many ways.

Both were doing so to satisfy their cravings, one to nourish the soul and the other to feed the body - however in both cases, a Universal Power provided their sustenance.

# CASE OF THE MISSING CAT

Riyadh 2006

A gesture I shall never forget. ------

Time is the most elusive commodity for many in today's age. Some have no time, while a few without realizing, can easily squander productive time; it is how an individual analyses one's life, to avail or to lose those precious hours of the day.

Once, while waiting at the airport, I noticed people's frustration at flight delays, as rightly so their valuable time was being challenged. Waiting, for that matter can be daunting anywhere. But this wait, with our own choice can be made befittingly interesting, by enjoying seeing the world go by, or at best to simply meditate; as this is easily done in the quietest chambers of the heart, discretely keeping the adrenal in check, while also not discrediting the twenty first century's best friend 'Facebook', which keeps us occupied and fully entertained at every breath.

All this came to my idle mind, half frustrated, while I stood at the airport for a few hours waiting for my son's arrival.

My parents probably went through similar plight to receive me driving long distances and then waiting for us. In later years, when my mother was having difficulty walking, she would still come, but wait in the car, holding a Tupperware, full of peeled oranges and sliced apples, which she had cut for me with her shaking hands. This love was indescribable - a love that encompassed everything.

Now, that my own children are grown up, I do the same thing, but opting for the easier version of taking bananas for them and myself. It simply was love that seemed to drive us to do so every time.

On one of our son's visits, he had informed us in advance that we should not trouble ourselves in this regard, and he will come home by himself.

We decided on this occasion to defer to him and found ourselves waiting to have dinner together.

The wait for me was long, aggravated further due to again - a flight delay. Just then, the doorbell rang, and I rushed towards the door to receive him. As we sat down around the dinner table to enjoy the meal, we found him very excited to tell us about his encounter on arrival and on his way home. In a persuasive tone, he shared a story, which had touched him deeply, and on hearing it, we too were moved beyond words.

This then is the story in his own words.

"My boss had asked me to feed his gold fish while he was away on a holiday; but here I was, returning from a weekend in Dubai having totally forgotten to feed them. I imagined that the fish had not been fed for two full days and I now feared the worst".

I had to somehow, convince a taxi driver to take me to the residential compound and wait, while I struggle through the tight security protocols; feed the fish, and then finally drop me home in the complete opposite end of the city; a complicated and near impossible request at the best of times".

"I approached a taxi driver; but 'fuhget- about-it' was the response."

"I asked another driver - but he wanted three times the prescribed fare. I quickly waved him away with a show of contempt".

"Things were not looking good for me until I heard a comforting voice from amidst the din in an amiable thick South Indian accent. When I told him, I had the fish to feed, his eyes lit up and he readily agreed to become a part of my minor humanitarian mission".

"There was silence for much of the drive, until the driver broke it first. What he had to say was not just a wonderful story of human compassion but it portrayed the very spirit of Ramadan."

"A few weeks earlier he had found himself standing in front of a Turkish restaurant on one scorching hot evening, when from the corner of one eye he saw a beautiful pure white long haired, Persian cat crawl out from under the car."

"He looked around to see if he could find its owners but to no avail. Immediately worried for the cat's safety he instinctively opened the door of his taxi - and much to his surprise - in hopped the frisky cat and curled up against the dashboard."

"Not sure what to do, he took the loveable feline to his home."

"What do you feed a hungry cat he asked himself"? He called a friend at a local veterinary clinic for some help and was promptly told that the cat would require special cat food. He set out to buy the food only to find that just one bag of dry cat food would cost SR 80 - far too much for his meagre monthly salary. Yet, without thinking twice, he bought two bags."

"Most taxi drivers in Saudi Arabia hail from the Sub-continent. They come in search of a better life and a chance to save enough so that they can send money home to an ailing parent or a young wife. Their children grow up without them, rarely getting a chance to see them grow."

"More often than not, they live in poor conditions, sharing the space with other people."

"Back at his apartment he placed three bowls on the floor beside his bed for food, milk, and water".

"Where does a cat sleep, he asked himself, He then folded his fleece blankets on his bed to fashion a small sleeping area for the cat".

"Thus he lay awake wondering how he would take care of this cat over the next few weeks, with such a grueling work schedule as his!"

"He himself slept the rest of the night on the floor".

"A couple of days later, he happened to be driving past the same Turkish restaurant, when he spotted a western couple who seemed lost and were wandering the pavement as if looking for something.

He screeched the car to a halt and jumped out wanting to know what the couple were looking for.

The couple turned out to be German. He asked, what they were they looking for to be overcome with happiness on hearing that they were trying to find their lost cat. As soon as he described the feline he had given shelter to, and how he had cared for it over the last few days, they insisted that he take them to the cat immediately.

With this they hopped into his taxi driver's car and were then driven to a dark, non-descript apartment building in the outskirts of the city. The German couple cautiously walked up a rickety flight of stairs, swatting away at annoying mosquitoes.

As they opened the thin wooden door and walked in to his small studio apartment; the cat looked up, and jumped from the bed, straight into the arms of the German woman; purring with excitement, and the woman sobbing and overcome with happiness.

The husband immediately pulled out his wallet and handed the taxi driver all the cash he had at the time - close to 5000 Saudi riyals - equivalent to over two months of the taxi driver's salary.

However, the driver refused to take any money and requested that they only pay for the fare to and from his apartment."

The story was to leave me speechless, and I too had tears in my eyes. My son went on to add,

"While driving home, I could not help but wonder how the stars had aligned; a poor driver, in a rich Muslim country to miraculously able him to help a desperate Christian couple find their beloved pet."

"I was also to wonder that if one can show compassion towards an animal, why then do we find it so difficult to express it for our fellow humans"?

"Even more remarkable; during Ramadan, it was an ordinary person who was to teach me in such a vivid manner a lesson in charity and humanity".

Sufi saints, like the great 13th-century Sufi poet Rumi held all existence and religions to be manifestations of the same Divine reality.

Here was a poor man, who despite the scarcity of resources in an increasingly material world was truly blessed with a spiritually enriched soul.

# WORTH THE DETOUR

"We make a living by what
we get, but we make a life
by what we give."

Winston Churchill

Saudi Arabia '79

It was a blazing hot day, the sun shining brightly bathing everything in a fiery orange and almost blinding glare. Trying to find a taxi from the holy city of Mecca to Riyadh with dozens of others looking for the same appeared a mission impossible.

This cosmopolitan city, which is so loved and venerated by Muslims the world over, is situated in the center of a valley of the Sirat Mountains. Mecca is a city that is alive all the time with its magnificent spiritual beauty.

As this place is teeming with pilgrims, as it was then, we had to make do with any vehicle that answered our request. Fortunately, we were able to avail one. However due to our luck there was no heating or air conditioning. One had to be acclimatized to the prevailing weather without any fuss. Yet to our surprise, it had a radio, but one which could be tuned to just two stations. The driver was listening to one.

However, we had everything one could then have wished for; the car was rolling along at a reasonable pace, with hot air blowing on our faces on this monotonous route to Riyadh. The journey was long and all of us were tired after a very fulfilling day in this blessed city.

We interrupted our driver who was engrossed in listening to the radio, to ask him to stop somewhere so that we could pick up some food.

He nodded faintly without saying anything. This driver knew that within the wilderness of this vast desert there was no rest area along this lonely route for miles.

Ten or fifteen minutes later, we noticed to our surprise that he took a detour, from the highway. We were surprised at this unusual turn on this otherwise straight route! We then noticed that he went just a kilometer or so off route, along the winding dusty unpaved road, marked by long deep ruts, which had been made by the repeated passage of his own vehicle.

Just a few dwellings appeared visible around where he was heading and we were later to realize, it was his village and he was the only one who owned a car in it.

Nabeel drove us to his modest Bedouin abode in his small village; saying, "We will stop at my place to have food." This was a total surprise! Though somewhat reluctant at first, we felt we had no choice, but to comply with his suggestion and encouraged by the sincerity in his tone.

He led us into the Majlis of his clean mud dwelling, where they welcome guests. In a deep voice said, 'Ahlan wa Sahlan', uttered in a deep sincere tone and in his frank and simple Bedouin manner, and to make us feel comfortable and settle down, Nabeel pointed towards the rectangular rock hard cushions placed along the perimeter of the Majlis beckoning us to sit. The only other object that was in this white washed room was a big 'Sheesha' with multiple pipes in a corner.

We attempted to make ourselves comfortable on the rough jute mat, feeling the unevenness and roughness of the ground underneath. The rugged simplicity in this atmosphere made us feel connected to Mother Earth. As a warm welcoming gesture, he lit the incense burner and the strong fragrance of the Oud filled the room, which was overpowering and unusual to our senses.

All this seemed to be a perfect definition that described Feng Shui so well; the Chinese practice of living in tune with nature, and its invisible forces which bind the universe harmoniously with humanity.

As I was about to sit down; Nabeel without looking at me, pointed his hand, towards the door of the adjacent room. He was clearly aware that I did not know Arabic.

The door was open and covered for privacy with a thick cloth hanging from the roof to the floor.

I went inside; a woman was standing to greet me; wearing a black Abaya with a veil covering her face. All I could see were her bright sparkling eyes and hands. She was genuinely happy to see me. That was obvious from the warm hug and the kisses she gave on my forehead. Of course, I did not see her full face.

I was curious to know who this person was who had just given me such a warm welcome, in the midst of nowhere.

Making me feel comfortable, she quickly went inside her small clean 'Open' kitchen. These simple people had this open concept, even back in those days. All living and sharing together, with their meagre belongings and earnings in that small space of two rooms.

With so much love, I could see her prepare a beautiful meal for us.

Famished by now, all we needed was food. The aroma of fresh cooked food was unbelievably appetizing. A cloth mat and steel plates were placed before us; along with a pile of steaming hot pilaff with nuts and olives, and lentil soup in a big earthenware pot; all served completely unexpectedly, in the middle of the desert.

While the men ate separately, his wife and I had our food in this other room. I noticed that when eating, every time she took a bite, she would lift her veil halfway. The twinkle in her eyes clearly showed her true happiness at seeing us.

When we finished our food, I said 'Shukran'. Thank God, I knew how to say thank you in Arabic. This little gesture of mine made her lift her veil and we both exchanged a hearty laugh. With this, I knew that she had become my friend; someone, who had so happily prepared all this food for us, knowing that we might never meet again.

After such a delicious meal, we started falling into a stupor and hoping that our host would offer us a place to rest our heads for a while. Thanks to the effect of the filling feast.

It was also almost 2 o'clock, perfect time for a siesta. However well rested and with our stomachs full, we were now in a rush to leave, but the wife insisted that we have Kahwa before we continue on our journey.

I must have had this drink several times, but this one was so special; that I remember it to this day, steaming hot and brewed with cardamom powder and honey. Nevertheless all this seemed to pale in comparison to the outpouring of their love which had brought tears to our eyes.

It was a meal to remember. What a spontaneous and heart-warming hospitality, with so much genuine warmth and compassion for strangers!

Some people survive on the meager uncertain earnings they eke out daily, barely able to meet their needs for food, let alone any other necessities. However with simple goodness in his nature, all he had thought of at that moment, when we had asked him to stop to get some food while he drove us, was how best to fulfill our need.

We certainly left this generous host's simple dwelling, reflecting deeply in wonder at the richness of simple generosity so beautifully portrayed by his gesture, and the goodness that dwelt in his heart. His spirit truly exemplified for us all - that which classifies a human being in simple terms a 'good'. It is indeed gratifying that we our blessed in our lives with savouring such experiences, from time to time. This is their deep embedded culture, which we so closely observed.

How I wish I could meet them again, as this would have been the start of a simple, but sincere friendship, where people meet and are drawn to each other without any prior motive.

We later continued the remaining 500 km of our journey back home to Riyadh, after the spiritually enriching experience of our visit to Mecca, crowned by this entirely unexpected and highly pleasant encounter with a family, which truly exuded 'Inner Light'.

"If you have much, give your wealth.
If you have little, give your heart."
Rumi

# BRIDE OF THE RED SEA

Spending almost a decade in the cosmopolitan coastal city of Jeddah; a city dating back to the times of the Nabataen trade, was, and still is, the entry port and gateway to Islam's holiest places for the pilgrims. Thinking about this lovely city, 'The Bride of the Red Sea", as it is known, invigorates me even now, as it did when I was living there, was established in the 6th century BC and has existed and thrived since then.

The pristine clear azure waters and abundant marine life of the Red sea was stunning! I collected some amazing shells and corals from this nature's underwater treasure trove. Having seen this reef, probably the most spectacular in the world, I never fail to be overwhelmed with joy and wonder, every time my mind travels back in time to those days when I was living in Jeddah.

I am also fortunate that at a young age, this city had provided me the privilege of visiting the holy sites of Mecca and Medina, the cities I love passionately and which people dream of and strive to visit throughout their entire lives.

Each visit was different. Sometimes it bought calmness and contentment, and yet more often a sense of fulfillment and a feeling of connectedness with the Creator.

On one of our visits to Mecca, which is just an hour's drive from Jeddah, we stopped at a signal whilst on our way. While the drivers foot still on the brakes, a young boy approached us, handing over boxes and bottles of water. For a moment, surprised and reluctant to accept them, but noticing that other boys too were distributing these boxes and bottles to every car that stopped at the signal, I accepted them. He was so intent and absorbed in his task, that I could not avail the opportunity to thank him.

I noticed that there were big cartons filled with such boxes on the sidewalk to which these boys had swift recourse in order to facilitate this activity by them.

It was then the month of Ramadan, and almost everyone was fasting from dawn to dusk.

As the time approached to break the fast; a serene quietness started to prevail; the orange yellow sun was fading and descending away ever so gracefully on the horizon, and shyly making its way for darkness to the stars and the moon, all glorifying the Creator.

On our approach to Mecca, as we drove past the Sirat mountains and through the old quarters, the sight and feelings are indescribable.

We drove in a gradual descent through the plutonic igneous rocks that are a home to old settlements. This was in itself an experience. Families have lived there for ages, upon this once active volcanic magma resided, that subsequently had calmed down to harden, some millennia ago.

As we drove close to our destination, the sight of the elegantly towering minarets started to be noticeable, while driving through the winding road.

Deep emotions gushed through me; my entire being, still and motionless with humility.

Finally, I found myself standing, in front of this revered site, which God Himself has declared sacred; the largest and the holiest; venerated by all.

A throng of pilgrims filled the outer courtyard moving around in contentment. Even amidst this hustle and bustle, a serene peace and calmness prevailed, on their clean and radiant faces, which held back, inside them a deep profound urge to come back.

Adding to the grace and beauty of this captivating spiritual environment, were hundreds of pigeons who keep flying as if in ecstasy, throughout the day welcoming God's revered guests. With great love and devotion, the pilgrims too sprinkle grain to feed them, often before they feed themselves. Flocks of grey coloured pigeons with specks of green could be seen all the time, hesitantly but joyfully descending to the ground, pecking away at the grains whilst anticipating the next shower of this feed, in this wide-open inspiring space.

These pigeons appearing to be dressed by nature in almost the same grey uniform; like their fellow pilgrims, all covered in white, also tended to serve the reminder that all beings are equal in this journey of life! No colour, caste, and status did them divide.

Every time I recall this ethereal visual sight, it never fails to bring feelings of continuous peace and joy, as it appeared to do so to every other passerby.

As the day slowly approached sunset, our eyes were glued to the watches on our wrists, as every ticking minute brought us closer to the ordained time.

This found us too in a rush to join the thousands of people. The sound of the muezzin's prayer call echoing from the minarets was generating myriads of emotions as we started to break our completed fast. The hazy rose tinted sky was now almost going into slumber, bringing peace at dusk.

In order to break our fast, we opened the boxes filled with dates, fruit and juices, which had been handed to us on our way. I thanked the boy at the signal, in my heart, and prayed for his prosperity; and realized the true import of the saying, "It should be one's good actions that prompt a person to pray for the doer."

This was a beautiful moment inside the Grand Mosque. It was quiet, far from the worldly life, as everyone was intent on breaking their fast with dates, and quenching their thirst with the miracle spring water Zam Zam. Many generous people were voluntarily distributing food to all the thousands of people present in the mosque, its courtyard and beyond; as well in the side alleys; rows upon rows. The food was served, eaten, and the place all cleared up and cleaned for the sundown prayers that follow; after the prayer call in just 15 minutes.

What a remarkable sight! And possible, only at this blessed place so venerated by all.

This is one of those moments that whichever way it is explained, one cannot visualize or comprehend this moment. It has to be seen to be experienced!

It struck me that while this generosity is present throughout the world, and possibly can be experienced elsewhere, but nothing like this, and on this scale; as inside the sanctum or its vicinity and on the roads.

While prostrating with deep humility I thanked the Almighty Divine for giving me the opportunity to witness, and honoured by this special experience with the greatest of profound humility and respect on my part, in this blessed sanctuary.

I was also fortunate to do the pilgrimage, the Hajj. But it was not until much later that I was to discover the distinct wisdom and spirituality behind it, connecting ourselves to the Universal Power and to return from the experience with a deep and resonating reminder of our continuous link with it, at all times; with every breath.

This was the place where Islamic history began. Muslims have been doing the pilgrimage for more than fourteen centuries. Many Christians go for pilgrimage to the Camino de Santiago in Spain, and the Jews to the Wailing Wall in Jerusalem. All connected and praying to the same Creator, but only in different ways.

It is my belief that God loves all His creation and is open and welcoming to all those desirous of connecting with Him. However, it is up to the seeker to activate this connection. The Transmitter is always alive but the receiver has also to be functional, receptive and tuned on their part. This can happen only when the inner heart is clean and alive.

# FROM THE TENT CITY

A door opens with a chance meeting.

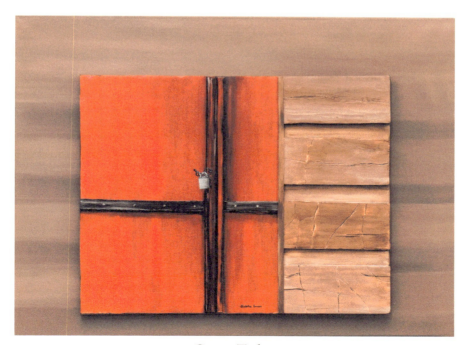

**Opens Today**
**The closed door highlights the clash of civilizations and the lack of dialogue**

My whole being was in a trance as I set my foot on the plains of Arafat; that occupy a very special place in Islam, as it was here that Prophet Mohammad (PBUH) gave his last sermon.

It was an extraordinary sight where millions of people - Yes, millions gather in a space, which is always able to hold them, to meditate, pray and repent.

During this spiritual journey the 'Hajj', we became acquainted with the Kureishy family. Both of us connected immediately, and our chance encounter later turned into a deep friendship. We spent the night together for performing another ritual in Mina, close to Mecca, under the open skies; one followed by all, regardless of the freezing nights of winter or the humid nights of summer. Here during that period, a sprawling tent city springs up, from the vast empty plains.

As much as could be expected during that time span, things were moving smoothly, with hundreds of thousands performing the same ritual, side by side during the same time, and the same day.

This was a phenomenally unusual sight, as that year, an estimated two million pilgrims were performing this sacred journey.

Continuing and looking forward to another fulfilling day in Mina, on a busy sun kissed bright day, close to early afternoon, Imran had left the camp to get some drinks and provisions for the elderly fellow campers, who were resting after late sleepless nights. Most were in deep meditation.

Maybe an hour later, we suddenly noticed unusual activity and noise in the vicinity, and thousands in frenzy. There was palpable sense of panic! No one knew what had happened. The only thing we saw and smelt was smoke, which was distinct and obvious, filling the air. With the gusts of wind, making it move faster and further. Visibility was limited.

My heart pounding, I was in a state of panic, fearing the worst, tears streaming down, and hardly able to hold my emotions back or control myself. Being all alone, I did not know where to go for help, and even, if I was brave, I was not sure if I would be able to come back to this location in that state of general chaos, where everyone is running around, worried about his own safety. Kureishy bhai, seeing my state, tried to comfort me, while preparing to go and see the situation.

As he was stepping out of the tent, he reassured me that he would look around all the avenues, visit the hospitals, and enquire from the police stations if necessary.

Though a little comforting, seeing someone around and volunteering to help a fellow pilgrim, I knew in my heart that at this point, all information desks would be focussing on the current emergency. I was also aware that the paramedics too would be anxious in managing the situation that had suddenly flared up.

It was now getting close to early evening; the smoke too was spreading further and filling up the entire area. It was thought that this unexpected fire which had erupted from one of the tents, had been caused by exploding gas cylinders; claiming many lives and had caused extensive damage. In spite of the local authorities managing and controlling large crowds and providing facilities for millions, still incidents keep happening.

After a very unsettling day, it was a great relief to see both arrive safely late that night. In that vulnerable, chaotic situation, it was difficult for them to find their way back to our camp, as during this period, the entire area looks similar, wherever the eyes travel.

While we heaved a sigh of relief on their safe return, our heart were to reach out for these families, struck by this tragedy and had lost their dear ones.

I am always, reminded of Kureshy Bhai's concern for us, even in the face of danger to himself, in that uncontrollable situation.

His out of the way gesture, has remained in our hearts since then, and pleasantly blossomed into a enduring friendship, and a delight to be nurtured with an air of comradeship.

Since both of us were settled in North America, we often had a chance to catch up with each other.

Kureishy bhai was a highly distinguished, charismatic man, who could mould the creative minds. He ran his own successful business out of Palo Alto, California. Their company had its operations globally. The rumours were that the company was going to announce some strategic initiatives to meet yet greater challenges.

His company had a big presence in the Middle East as well. An ambitious visionary, with presence and enormous energy, he was instrumental in winning large contracts for his company in the region. After a phenomenal journey to success, he wanted to slow down because of his deteriorating health. As he was still winning business, he was now looking for someone to take care of his regional operations.

It seemed that while talking to us one evening, he had made up his mind as who he thinks would be a perfect fit for managing this new office. Just a few days later, Imran received an offer letter! A month following it, we were back in the Middle East.

# PRICELESS

Beautiful, unanticipated moments, were unexpectedly, unfolding in my life.

A day before travelling to Riyadh, I was busy with my preparations, doing last minute packing, organizing, and tending to various odd tasks around the house.

Although with time constraints, among other things, I had to tidy the house before leaving.

Strange as it may sound, that particular day and moment, a quick glimpse of the room, which I have been seeing and living for the last 22 years, made me reflect upon my surroundings.

I paused, and stood motionless to sense a distinct moment of realization.

I sat down. It was just so quiet. I could even decipher the chirping of the birds, though their language was unknown to me, still the sound were so familiar. I fleetingly looked around at the collection of some old handcrafted object d'arts in the room that almost often took me down the memory lane.

Almost as if in the footsteps of Marco Polo, I had explored many places that had sparked my curiosity and interested me in acquiring the vintage pieces that speak for themselves. Some of them hold substantial history behind them, unveiling how much we have evolved, and still, can go further beyond.

With introspection, there was a serious dialogue with my inner self.

Though I had a passion for collectibles, I now felt, that one thing I had not sought, and found no quest or urge in me for acquiring, would henceforth become the most important yearning to possess for me.

This was a piece of the Kiswa, the black silk covering of the Kabah, the cube-shaped stone structure, built by Prophet Abraham. It is the epicenter for Muslims all over the world, and the direction towards which they all pray. I, as well as thousands of others revere the Kiswa; as it is blessed by being in close harmony with the Kabah.

I had the good fortune to attend an exhibition at the Riyadh museum, and to see closely some of the most talented artisans passionately and reverently embroidering the Kiswa, in gold thread and adorning it with verses from the Quran in preparation for dressing the Kaaba during the annual Hajj pilgrimage.

While I had this keen desire to acquire, even if a small piece of this revered cloth, but did not know how to go about it.

Things take their own course. We were now back in in the Middle East for a few years assignment.

After settling down, I wanted to get in touch with a few old friends, specially my Palestinian neighbour, Imtiaz with whom I almost have a soul connection. As soon as she came to know that I was in town, we received a very compelling warm dinner invitation.

On that occasion, their whole family was to join us. Interestingly our friendship and connection is still the same, even now, she talks to me in Arabic and I reply her in English. Yet both of us have always understood each other so well throughout, as if on a higher plane of communication, that it is unbelievable. How we can follow the conversation, is still a beautiful mystery to this day.

Time seems to have stood still for Imtiaz. She is a beautiful woman in the inner and outer sense, illuminated face, and sparkle in her eyes; a true embodiment of kindness and generosity at its very best.

After a very enjoyable evening with their whole family and a sumptuous dinner, we were together in the same car, all heading home.

While driving back, I found Imtiaz to be quiet and seem little bit tired, as she had been volunteering outside the country, for the past month; helping the injured and suffering women and children, carrying food, clothing, blankets and other necessities and arranging clean water for the displaced families in the war torn areas in that region.

She had appeared, clearly distressed and heartbroken while talking about the stories of separation. As some left their elderly parents and family behind adjusting to the new unsettled environment, not to mention the trauma, that the past provokes in the present.

During our conversation in the car, Imtiaz asked us to accompany her to their house first, as she wants to present a gift; something that is very special and certainly will be precious to me.

We were a little reluctant to agree, as it was well past midnight; but at their insistence, we accompanied her. After a long interval, I was entering the welcoming space that was so familiar to me. Mirrored panels adorned the ornate lavish hall. The repositioning of the rich antique, carved console table was noticeable on one wall, while the other adorned with family portraits, with a addition of a few new young faces was a testimony to this gracious charming family who lived here.

As always, their house was immaculate and spotlessly clean. I could even sense this in the dark! We followed her to the dining room as she opened the lights. The bohemian crystal chandelier sparkled above the lacquered, mahogany dining table.

I was simply reminiscing about the past filled with vignette of memories, admiring the room, where we had frequently sat so often and spent happy moments together, enjoying her home made gourmet meals,

Upon coming out of my reverie, I noticed that she had gone up the stairs, holding carefully, her full-length dress, the 'Jalabiya', just a few inches above her feet. She looked amazing wearing that royal blue colour. At seventy, she was still so robust and energetic.

With a smile on her face, she came back running on the grey-carpeted stairs without holding on to the banisters, carrying with her scissors and the folded grey silk embroidered cloth.

The speed with which she was coming down, had me worried that she may slip or fall.

It was a moment, which had held so many emotions of anticipation; a sense of mystery combined with feelings of mutual love and an expression of gratitude on my part for the present I was to receive.

With an air of reverence, she made me unfold the silk cloth, on her dining table.

I was simply mesmerised at what I saw - It was a piece of the Kiswa!

This was beyond my wildest dreams!

I was ecstatic, wonderstruck, and felt truly blessed. With all these emotions coursing within me, I started to shiver as I felt a close connection to the 'House of God', the Kaaba and the Divine, One and Only.

None could have known that I had a very strong inner urge to acquire such a treasure, only a few days earlier, and here it was all happening right in front of my eyes! Even though I was holding it in my hand, yet I could not believe. It was a big piece of the Kiswa with woven Quranic inscriptions. Imtiaz asked me to cut it from the center. With shaking hands, I did. I was in a flux of emotions; nervous, excited and in a spiritual trance. I had to be careful that I did not cut across the inscriptions that were so beautifully woven into the silk cloth. These inscriptions in gold thread and black silk were so congruent to the mystic and spiritual nature of the Kiswa itself.

Surprised at why she did not give it or desire to keep it for her own children – Imtiaz gave me a big warm affectionate hug saying in response; "Remember! Things only go to the recipient who desires it passionately." ."This was just meant for you". At this, tears welled up in my eyes and just could not believe that I was actually holding it!

With this desire and yearnings of mine fulfilled in this miraculous manner, I could not thank God enough. It had been the answer to my earnest prayers and my deepest wish and dream, at the time coming to life.

"Nearly all the best things that came to me in life, have been unexpected, unplanned by me."

Carl Sandberg

This is so true!

# DESERT BREAD FEST

I had tears in my eyes listening to him --- His actions were simply touching, humane and sublime.

Sometimes, events happen that are out of the ordinary, inexplicable, and leave a deep impact. Madinah has a rich history and a special significance and importance. Each time it has been a wonderful experience in different ways, but always serene and full of blessings.

I have had the privilege of visiting this radiant, sacred city of Madinah often, which is in the northwestern region of Saudi Arabia. I simply love this place! - A place on earth and in my heart, where all my sensory faculties are instantly awakened by a blissful spiritual connection.

Once we arrived in Madinah during the early hours of the morning, passing through Abu Zar Ghaffari street and similar old alleys, where distinct nostalgia still prevails in some parts, with small vendors sitting comfortably on the ground, selling 'Tasbeeh's', (prayer beads) and prayer mats, even in the wee hours of the morning.

As soon as I set my eyes on the main portal of the sanctuary, I could not wait for my last few minutes to go inside. With one the most overwhelming feelings of inner peace and indescribable calmness, we entered the courtyard of the Grand mosque to offer our prayers. Its a breathtaking sight to behold, with all its glory. The spiritual atmosphere was noticeable all around, the green lights from the tall minarets were radioing their own charm and welcome, as the dawn, waiting to spread its brightness in this sacred city.

It was probably 5:30 in the morning, a beautiful, quiet, serene moment to meditate. I was in a state difficult to comprehend and equally difficult to describe. The phrase, "I'm in seventh heaven" pretty much could be close to describe this feeling; even if not in its totality but close. Most of us do not know, nor can I imagine what this station would be like? However, I earnestly believe, if one wishes to experience it, we would have to endeavour towards it, and walk the walk and talk the talk.

After a very fulfilling long day, we were tired and simply wanted to have a quick meal and retire. The food court near our hotel, filled with ongoing pilgrims, young and old, and the fast food chains bustling, catering food for the pilgrims who had come to seek food for their soul.

The food that these people serve is simple, fresh, and tantalizing to the taste buds. Many upscale hotels surround this place, fully catering all cuisines, serving extravagant breakfast buffets - a feast that is an early morning treat after the night's meditation.

This has always been a very busy place, as pilgrims keep coming in and going, throughout the day. Madinah draws people from all over the world, being the most sacred destination of pilgrimage after Mecca.

It was always exciting to meet a cross section of the cosmopolitan world and with some; we often had very enlightening discussions. Although on most occasions, we did not know the people from before, but somehow, there seemed to be a connection, and a strong bond, a feeling of oneness and brotherhood. This was possibly because everyone was coming here with the same devotion. What came across was the fact, that every human being has the milk of kindness in his heart and at its core, a deep sense of humanity.

We were in the city for almost the whole week. On the day of our arrival, just as we had finished our dinner, there was still some leftover bread on our plates. We noticed a middle-aged man, his head covered in woven cane skullcap, visiting all tables with a lowered gaze but with eyes wandering. He diffidently approached us holding a large plastic bag, and in a soft voice asked us, if we could give him our leftover bread. The man was unkempt wearing ordinary clothes, unshaven, expressionless face, and meek in demeanour.

We of course readily agreed.

It was heart rendering, and I thought how desperate one could get for food, going around like this, and begging everyone for scraps.

While we were picking up our belongings and planning to leave, we could not help noticing that he was still going around and requesting everyone sitting at the tables.

At first, we did not think much about this, but, as we went to this place frequently, we started observing this happening every day, and noticed that he was filling the large bag he carried only with bread. He kept the filled bag in the corner, and while holding another empty bag, he kept an eye for new customers who entered the food court. This was an unusually busy place all day, and seemed like a cross between a place for rest, reflection as well as for seeking sustenance for both the body and soul.

We realized that so much bread could not just be for himself or his family. Intrigued, and our curiosity getting the better of us, one evening, we ventured to ask him, what he did with all bread that he collects.

The story that unfolded touched me deeply, and reaffirmed my faith in the inherent kindness and compassion in man. It strengthened the feelings that we had been experiencing about the oneness of humanity.

Initially, he seemed a little reluctant to reveal his mission; but slowly opened up and said, that he collected the bread to feed a herd of goats and camels in the middle of the desert.

He was reluctant to say further, but my curiosity did not allow him stop there. In a low voice, as if embarrassed to go on, he told us, he travels deep into the desert everyday to find these stray animals, which really were not part of any herd, or owned or tended by any shepherd. They sometimes have nothing to eat, and many die as a result.

I was staring at him in bewilderment, in awe and at something, I could not have imagined. I was wonderstruck listening to this astonishing story. He had taken upon himself, this task of being a conduit and a means of providing sustenance to the hungry animals.

Madinah is an oasis in the desert, surrounded by volcanic mountains and rocky terrain that date back to the first geological period of the Paleozoic era. As expected, there is not enough wild vegetation or shrubs, let alone verdant greenery in the arid desert environment. There are only stretches of flat, wide desert and hillocks, with no shade in sight for miles, with the scorching heat during the summers reaching up to a searing 50 degrees C and low temperatures in the winters, dipping down to single digits.

Animals, such as camels, which are the fauna of the desert, have to forage over long distances to feed themselves.

Considering the harsh desert climate, I was amazed at this man; admiring his courage and resilience, as I reflected on how he willingly undertakes this hard and demanding task daily - by recognizing their need, and his urge to help, made him collect bread to feed them and his deep desire to alleviate their hunger, in such a selfless manner.

His ability to suppress his ego to a level that enabled him to go around asking people for their leftovers, day in and day out, was truly a cause for wonder. It was heartwarming and inspirational, to say the least, to see the duty this man had taken upon himself.

I had tears in my eyes listening to him. To me, his actions appeared to be just a small demonstration of his compassion for all of creation.

I thought to myself, that my prayers are not the only way to get connected to my Creator. Recognizing the needs of others, and reaching out to them selflessly was also a route that further helped in attaining this objective.

This simple man and his actions led to a much deeper insight - true humanity and its service with a sense of duty is all about putting others - even animals, above self.

It forcefully struck me that this person was but a "Shepherd" who was a conduit for providing sustenance to His "Flock," and that God has predetermined and decreed the sustenance of every soul.

# THE BIG MOVE

Canada 1996

As time went by, we approached a juncture when our children began to enter a different phase of life. We felt this was imperative and one of those pivotal moments, that called for us to embrace change; and to move on.

We migrated to this lovely country Canada in the late nineties, crossing the big puddle - The Atlantic, excited to embark on a northern journey. At some point, we all go through some kind of metamorphosis, not unlike the transformation of a caterpillar to a butterfly.

As with any adventure, through mountains, valleys and rivers, one can also face a rollercoaster.

As many immigrants have experienced, it is not always an easy transition to leave the relaxed and comfortable life of the Middle East, and move to a fast paced, ever changing Western society.

It was here, I began to learn that life has vicissitudes, and challenges that I had not encountered in my previous years.

Also realizing, that in every good phase of life, it was the benevolence of God's will, and every challenging phase too was God's will.

He controls everything that happens in our lives, in spite of our calculated decisions.

As the saying goes, "Man proposes and God disposes".

In the words of Albert Einstein -

> "Everything is determined, the beginning as well, as the end, by forces over which we have no control. It is determined for insects, as well as for the stars. Human beings, vegetables or cosmic dust, we all dance to a mysterious tune, intoned in the distance by an invisible piper."

The day I arrived in Toronto, it was Minus 32° C. Upon landing the immigration officer very politely asked me, "Ma'am, where are you coming from?" After a sixteen hour-long flight, my instant answer was "From the oven to the freezer." I certainly did make him laugh. When I bumped into him sometime later, I was amused to discover that he still remembered my spontaneous reply.

With a white carpet welcome and a piercing wind, we stepped out into the snow-clad city with the freezing temperatures of the North, grey gloomy skies, mounds of snow on both sides, majestically paving a way for us to embark on our new journey. Our so-called warm clothes were not warm enough, and had to be upgraded to something Down filled; sooner than later. The temperatures too, kept reminding me, albeit forcefully to be aware of the chill factor. A phrase I learnt and felt simultaneously, for the first time.

This was a big country move. Shall I say, from one continent to another, from an easy paced, historically rich Middle East to a vibrant, progressive, North America?

The environment was not completely alien to me, as I had been visiting these places earlier, experiencing their culture, enjoying their culinary delights, and meeting some wonderful people on the way; who influenced and enriched my thinking and from which I effortlessly gained tremendous inspiration, and which has captivated me immensely ever since.

As with any move or change, one faces new situations, challenges. It certainly takes time to understand and adapt to the demands of the new life.

> "Life is like riding a bicycle, to keep
> your balance, you must keep moving."
>
> Albert Einstein

**With Hazel McCallion, one of Canada's longest-serving Mayors.**

**My tribute to Canada on behalf of 192 immigrant nationalities and 71 Aboriginal groups on its 150th anniversary, represented in the small squares made of the iconic Maple tree wood, and the Maple leaf engraved on pewter.**

# SUBMISSION

I thought my involvement in Art would make me feel legitimately good as this being something I consistently enjoy and admire, yet certain realities kept me from pouring my heart and soul into my work for a certain time. This period in my life was marked by the deteriorating health of my parents who were the treasures of my life. I was deeply concerned; to say the least and it was an overwhelming experience.

Both of them passed away within a matter of two months. This was an irreplaceable loss and I was inconsolable. Each coming day was a replay of all the events and of our cherished moments. They were an integral part of my identity and when I lost them, I felt like they took a part of me with them. The legacy that my parents left me was phenomenal. Such was their stature that people remember them to this day with the deepest respect.

My immersion in the arts had introduced me to some good friends, whom I used to meet occasionally. One of them, on seeing me, somehow noticed and sensed that I was in low spirits. Nour, the good friend that she was, felt that I needed emotional strength and company to cheer me up.

One late afternoon, I was all by myself, reading Andrew Harvey's 'Teachings of Rumi", a remarkable collection encompassing Rumi's most luminous mystical poetry, portraying the balance between love for God, and following the path of discipline, which God has set forth to achieve Divine Spirituality.

My reverie was disturbed by the doorbell ringing at a time, when I was almost in a bubble; transported to another world of the inner heart - a fragrant rose garden. Though difficult to leave the book at this beautiful juncture, I quickly ran to open the door and was pleasantly surprised to see Nour, with her same infectious smile, radiating her familiar warmth and friendliness. She had driven a long distance to spend a few quality hours with me. I was touched beyond words by her visit, which was so uplifting. She had come at a point in my life when I had needed the emotional support to regain my vigour and vibrancy.

> "'One of the signs and tasks of true friendship
> is to listen compassionately to the hidden silences -
> They lie concealed in the silence between the words or
> in the depth of what is unsayable between two people."
> John.O'Donohue

Nour and I sat down and had a heart-to-heart conversation, with plenty a time at our disposal. All that we needed was a perfectly brewed cup of tea. I quickly got up, as I wanted to serve her in a way to really make her feel special.

I laid out the Belgian tablecloth, so meticulously embroidered by Ammi and with a lighter heart; we enjoyed our tea with its invigorating aroma. Luckily, two slices of the Sacher torte were still lying in the fridge. I was so happy that she liked it. This exotic delicacy just melted in her mouth and left her in ecstasy. Who would not love this cake, as it is arguably the most famous cake in the world, crafted almost a century ago in 1832. Our indulgence in chocolate patisserie is a legacy of our visit to Vienna, where we were introduced to the delights of the Viennese pastries and confectionery.

Everything was there for the perfect cup of tea, except for Ammi's blessed presence,

> "Drink your tea slowly and reverently, as if it is
> the axis on which the world, earth revolves
> slowly, evenly, without rushing toward the future,
> live the actual moment. Only this moment
> is life."
> Thich Nhat Hach

The sunset created the ambiance to long for a second cup as the sky's blue and orange palette adorned the horizon, giving us tidings and a chance to avail the blessings of yet another day. Splashes of colour elaborated the elegance of the tulips and daffodils, elevating my spirits and changing my mood.

Nour's gesture was a perfect example of a genuine friend; a true reflection of the phrase, "Tea and Sympathy.

Before leaving, it seemed she had something profound to share.

As I was about to open the door, Nour paused while looking at me, saying in a soft tone, "We all have to surrender to the will of God," and how right she was! Her words, seemed to convey the same continuation of the thought of 'Divine love and Submission' in the book I was reading; but these same words, I was now hearing, as if a complex theory was being explained to me to ponder at the right moment.

To fully comprehend the concept of surrender is one thing; but to actually experience a situation and then to surrender, is what is challenging. I must have surrendered countless of times with great conviction and good intention, yet the struggle had continued in my inner self. It is said, 'Time is a big healer'; so I believe is one's state of surrender.

However sincere the intention, it is, at most times very trying and testing. Nevertheless, the realization gradually starts taking over. Well! One has no choice, but to surrender consciously to the will of our Creator, leaving just everything to Him, while working towards them and yet hoping for freeing oneself. Though it is heartening to realize, as at most times, the worries just do not disappear, but it is then that faith, which gives patience and resilience in the face of adversity.

There is a change within, settling quietly- to be felt later, or to a few - never; and unknowingly the softer side slowly starts taking precedence, the blessedly new patience, perseverance and humility. The truth is; nothing holds these virtues back, as these beautiful traits, little by little, unhurriedly sink in over time, in becoming one's part, and sometimes unconsciously starts to radiate the same energy to other lives around us. Somehow, our approach to life changes in an incomprehensible way, leading to a calm state of peace and contentment. The ultimate key simply lies in absolute love for our Creator and complete belief in the 'Power of the Almighty'.

"On the still calm waters of surrender,
the reflections of clarity appear."
Bryant McGill

There is always something good in store - much beyond our expectations, or even our imagination. All one needs is a powerful motivation and a passion to strive towards future goals.

"To accomplish great things, we must
not only act, but also dream; not only
plan but also believe."
Anatole France

# FAITH IN GOD

Toronto

Every chance meeting, 'Profound and Insightful'.

The ever so glorious cascading seasons dictate a regime for work and leisure year after year. The streets that earlier glistened with a white snow blanket were now slushy and slippery, gradually melting away, displaying a whole new look, as the last traces of the ice necklace on the windows and the roof, subtly start to melt away drop by drop, allowing the rain to take its turn .

As now with the dawn of the new day and the sun's brilliance, familiar yet so different, the tiny leaves start to smile on the trees and the snow-clad grass comes smiling out of hibernation, crisp and green. The much awaited spring is felt everywhere, offering plenty to look forward to, with newly harvested fresh air, yielding novel opportunities and motivation to many.

The days stretch out, with late majestic sunsets to look around and for some, to find a property of their dreams.

On one such late evening, I received a phone call from a client, requesting me to set up an appointment for home staging, prior to the listing of their house. My company, 'The Finishing Touch', was introducing the concept of home staging for the first time in Canada.

By being in this creative arena, I had established some good contacts. Many of these had developed into friendship that would last a lifetime.

I enjoyed working with a few, especially Naz and Saeed. Though I did not know, that with Naz I would nurture my spiritually along the way. They were very cooperative, which made things easy and enjoyable most of the time. As the world of design can be overwhelming, I had to synchronize my creativity with their personal style. Over a period this became more than a business relationship.

I enjoyed visiting their new home and loved her company. Every time I went to see her, I did something for them, which they really loved. Sitting in her living room, we exchanged endless anecdotes and of course serious conversation too. It was refreshing listening to her talking so eloquently, and at the same time thought provoking. Her tender sensitive words were full of wisdom, always making sense. It was like talking to an encyclopedia, current and fresh and in-depth; food for thought, after each visit.

Over time, I was to come to admire her innate calmness and the great sense of contentment in her entire being, which I attributed to her undeniably strong faith in God. With infectious optimism, and unbridled courage to fight various battles inside her, she was progressive in her approach to life, yet her firm belief was, that things take their own course and the resulting outcome was always in the hands of God.

Naz Apa was always thankful for everything the Creator had given her, and all that has happened to her in different phases of her life, regardless of her certain unfortunate circumstances, which she shared with me.

Her strength and complete faith in God made me ponder, and developed in me an urge to have the same powerful belief in myself.

She was an astonishingly radiant woman with a certain 'Je ne sais quoi'; an indefinable pleasing quality she possessed and by which she related, with unmistakable authenticity and love. Our chemistry was undeniable. I found in her a mother in absentia.

Invariably, whenever we met, I implored her to remember me in her prayers. With a smile on her face, she would give me the simple answer "Just have faith in God".

Most often, my request to her pray for me came naturally without any thought. However, her answer was always the same "Have faith in God." I started seriously reflecting upon this request of mine, and her mystic yet undoubtedly sagacious response to me.

Her love made me and my family visit them frequently.

Availing a bright sunny weekend, we once decided to pass by their house for a quick visit, to pay our respects. I actually enjoyed her company, and I felt that she enjoyed mine. The visit was so refreshing. Naz Apa and Saeed bhai were always happy to see us. Visiting them was like going to your parents house; relaxed and unpretentious.

We had another thought provoking conversation as we sat on her new garden chairs in the open patio, overlooking a small park, as we sipped cold lemonade, which she had freshly squeezed for us with a dollop of honey. The background Sufi soundtrack of the legendary Abida Perveen she had put on for us had to compete with the sound of the construction activity in a nearby development.

In her company, we had lost track of time. I immediately stood up to hug her, as we begged her leave.

Just as I was about to sit in the car; I heard her say, "See you soon."

I found myself quite hesitant to say anything, though in my heart, the desire to request her to pray for me was still there.

We exchanged a deep meaningful glance, and before the car rolled on, with a natural grin, she drew close to me, recognizing my thoughts and, whispered, "I always remember you in my prayers." I smiled. The contentment on her face on seeing me was apparent. She knew that her words had begun to sink in. "Have faith in God," echoed in me. It still reverberates to this day.

Our friendship was not a mere coincidence, but something that was "Meant to be," to help inculcate this very basic trust and strong belief in God. It is strange that I must have heard this so often from so many people before, but it took just one person, who with her certain grace, left an imprint of her personality in a way which implanted and infused the good message of belief, and which she did so gracefully and subtly by simply re-emphasizing it the right time, every time.

"The moment in between what you once were, and who you are now becoming, is where the dance of life really takes place."

Barbara De Angelis

# ARTFULLY YOURS

Toronto

There is certainly a reason for everything - We were in the settling in phase; excited to start afresh in a completely new environment in Canada, with different circumstances and new acquaintances.

When someone visited us, it was quite an occasion; as we hardly knew anybody then.

The Consul General of the country of my birth was starting his new assignment to my adopted country. An enigmatic, yet charming personality; he had an extensive knowledge of the arts and a passion for collecting artifacts.

Their visit to our abode proved to be a blessing in disguise. While having tea, our honoured guest's eyes happened to rest on the Chinese porcelain bowl placed on the center table.

This had somehow caught his attention!

I had painted it a few years back and had embellished it with calligraphy in the Kufic script. I had been particularly keen to paint this angular, vertical style, as this was the first formal script that originated in the Hijaz region of the Arabian peninsula.

The embassy at that time was looking for someone from the community to represent the country at the prestigious

Royal Ontario Museum. He at that moment instantly thought of me. Wow! My eyes lit up in awe. Instead of accepting this lovely offer without hesitation, I demurred, saying, "I have no suitable credentials to represent in a place so well admired and respected."

However, not accepting my initial modest response and stressing that he recognized my potential, said, "You have to prepare your own credentials". "Start transferring your thoughts on canvas, and go in for a solo exhibition".

This was the exciting beginning of my journey on the creativity train!

Upon receiving this encouraging and motivating advice, I found myself eager to push the envelope and start preparing for the solo exhibition as suggested. Surprisingly there was the creation of sixty pieces of artwork in less than two years. However, I find it is always difficult to part with my paintings; as intense love and feelings are inevitably poured into them, as they become a part of one.

My two solo exhibitions; the latter in 2012 were very well received by both art enthusiasts and the public at large. The President of York University, Mamdouh Shoukri and its previous President Lorna Marsden, as well as Deep Saini, then the Vice President University of Toronto, where my children studied, graced the occasion. I greatly admire them as being such accomplished yet humble people, who not only create a legacy for themselves, but also stay true to their passion. We later became friends, bringing inspiration and joy to my life.

**Imran and myself with Mr. Mamdouh Shoukri, then President and Vice Chancellor, York University**

**With Prof. Deep Saini, then Vice President University of Toronto and Mr. Brian Musselwhite, curator Royal Ontario Museum**

**With the Hon. Lorna Marsden, Ex President and Vice-Chancellor, York University**

**A panaormic view of my Solo exhibition**

While channeling my creativity, I realized that:

"An artist is no other than he who unlearns
what he has learned in order to know himself"-
This is a perfect and apt definition of what it
means to be an artist."
E.E.Cummings

The paintbrush allows me to express spontaneously my thoughts, and to present a conceptual view of the colorful tapestry of experiences that in themselves are an inspiration; and the outpouring of my inner self. This I feel is present in the finished work and the embodiment of all the beauty that surrounds us. These artistic outpourings have the ability to represent and transform not only ourselves but also have an impact on the world around us. This is one of the reasons, why artists of all genres share the values to highlight universal issues with their unique style, be a neophyte or an accomplished artist.

"Your eyes not only see everything around you as
is, but also project what you wish to look in this world".
"Our eyes are our conduit to our mind and heart."
Pemmaraju

The play of light and shadows has always fascinated me, be it in my own work or noticeable elsewhere. It has the power to evoke positivity, even the thought of it brings brightness and energy and the connection with the Inner Light that resides in us all.

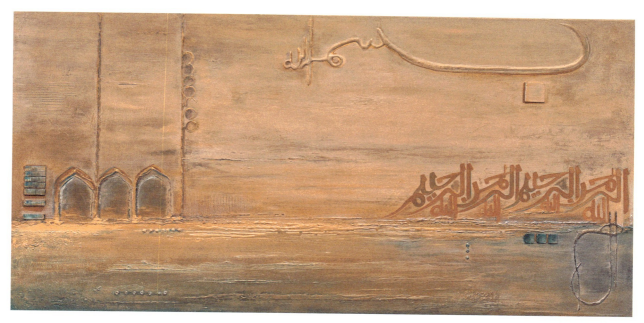

Sabiha Imran

**"Luminosity" - Acrylic on Canvas**

While on a museum run, I had a chance to observe this effect of light at Amsterdam's Rijks Museum in the paintings of the famous Dutch master Rembrandt, and Claude Monet, the 18th century French artist, where the effect is so brilliantly portrayed; and a moment to appreciate the spiritual dimension, in the paintings of Vincent Van Gogh, the famous post impressionist painters longing to connect with the Creator.

> "The artists chose unmediated spiritual
> path, through mystical experiences. The
> feeling of connecting with a deeper reality;
> a power much greater than ourselves."
> Curator Lochnan

Artists all over have been expressing their feelings and thoughts through different mediums, even through 'Visio Divina', Latin for divine seeing. Surely, divine, since it emanates from the heart and seen by the eyes, which in itself is a process of creation.

Furthermore, inspiration can come in any form, at any place, triggered almost instantly by the most mundane of things. I on my part have found that many a times it was my evening walk, which launched me on my creativity train.

Philosopher and poet Friedrich Nietzsche writes, "All truly great thoughts are conceived by walking."

The serenity of a quiet walk is in harmony with the humming and chirping of the birds and the retreating sunshine; and in unison with the calming gentle breeze, ever so quietly meander through the burnished trees. My gentle strides echo on the thick carpet of grass; crunching and crushing it; pleasantly releasing its fresh scent with every step; an invitation for me to walk over it again and providing this blissful environment to contemplate.

The bustling exhibition spaces too, inspires and encourages me on the extraordinary ideas expressed in great compositions in a completely different contemporary environment, providing a stimulating platform to engage in conversations with the curators and multi- disciplinary artists, sharing their creative perspective; and a chance to experience innovations in an ever-changing landscape.

One such place is the annual Art Fair, at Toronto's Convention Centre, where together with inspiration; I experienced an amazing coincidence, a chance meeting with a charismatic artist, Esther Bryan. She seemed bold and full of ideas yet sensitive, whose inner light truly shines through her vision. Strolling and admiring the works along one aisle, I noticed, we both were viewing the same canvass. Her concentration and focus was clearly apparent.

The space was full of energy and burst of colour; enhanced with sunshine filtering serenely from the expansive glass walls and without choice, the downtown's skyscrapers become a backdrop, which seemed to compliment the human creativity inside. This was almost a pre-nuptial scene, with artists, prancing on stools, fixing and adjusting, craning their necks and stretching their arms to arrange the canvases, and their eyes searching for perfection, and a real ultimate look.

Esther was here to attend this event and had come all the way from Williamstown, a small Ontario town that overlooks the calm Raisin River. I have driven past this green peaceful area, which is famous for the annual foot race. One can well imagine how her creativity must have blossomed in such a tranquil location, with wild grapevines, laden with grapes, growing along the shores of the river.

I was fortunate to have met this extraordinary individual and enthusiastic artist at that year's art extravaganza. We had a casual conversation while viewing another art installation, sharing the thought, 'Art should not just be displayed on the walls; but should resonate with some meaningful message and purpose.'

As I reminisced on my life's journey, this lovely artist also shared her story with me, which in some way became part of my own journey. I found that I could relate very well with her. Our lives, roles, and passions were similar; as mothers, wives, daughters and artists; and then, immigrants as well. Though each one of us has a different way of expression; our past, our background, together with our creativity gave us a rather unique dimension.

After the Iron curtain in Europe had collapsed, Esther, along with her father had revisited Slovakia after decades in order to meet their loved ones they had left behind.

She openly shared the questions that came to her mind. Why did she felt so connected, though meeting her paternal side of the family after such a long interval? How people still can be so similar, in spite of being in different cultures and environment and having different lifestyles and experiences? With these searing thoughts in her mind, she was to confide that she often wondered where she belonged in the fabric of life. She deemed every human soul irrespective of their colour and creed, unique in this tenuous thread of existence, with a longing to belong, and be accepted, which she believes is 'A Place for all'.

With these rich thoughts, incalculable stitches, and countless hours of research, coupled with complete faith and vision, she had launched a unique textile art project, 'The Quilt of Belonging'. It was certainly daunting and challenging, but became a passion with her and an invitation to all to participate and belong.

Who could have refused such a compelling invitation! I accepted immediately, as this collaborative effort was to become Canada's first textile artwork. It is now included in the Canadian curriculum to promote cultural understanding and celebrate common humanity and compassion.

This monumental quilt is 120 feet long, consisting of 263 blocks joined; the way humanity ought to be connected; with compassion for all, transcending all boundaries.

I was near completion of the block, when Esther visited to see my progress. While sharing her vision, I too managed to glimpse into the real side of her being. Her compassion and faith were unbelievable.

Without enough funds, workspace, fabric, materials and neither even a sewing machine, nor a table or work surface; as well as not knowing how to approach a grant, she still carried on. All this seemed to her like "Going to Mars" Adding, "I gradually came to understand that this was to be a work of faith." "I had experienced God's provision for my family; and firmly believed that nothing is impossible for Him."

With such humble beginnings, and only in a few years, the journey of the quilt is now well recognized. I am proud to be part of this iconic and groundbreaking project of hers. The privilege of having contributed a block for a country where I spent almost two decades of my life was by itself rewarding enough for me. For this symbolic work expresses the world's need for unity and tolerance, truly representing the essence of Canadian values.

Esther's vision had touched me to the core; for it explained that everyone is equal in the tapestry of life, and we can touch the hearts of others through compassion and help. This is really 'Inner Light'.

There are many divisive forces around the world; yet despite what may look like a win for some, the world still manages to stay together. It is so because the forces of cohesion and unity are much stronger. The collective convictions are winning and will win in the end.

**A panoramic view of the Quilt of Belonging, displayed in the Museum of Civilization, Ottawa**

The spirit behind the "Quilt of Belonging" is so aptly conveyed in a couplet by an Urdu poet, Makhdoom Mohiuddin,

> Hayat lay kay chalo, Kai'naat lay kay chalo
> Chalo tou saray zamanay ko saath lay kay chalo

English translation

> Take life with you, Take Universe with you
> As you move, take the whole world with you

**Esther Bryan pointing at my block**

# LIGHT STROKES

The feeling of compassion kept echoing in me from unexpected directions and unusual events in life.

The summer breaks prompted my parents, who were nature and heritage lovers, to travel up north on the famous Karakorum Highway, the exotic historic ancient silk route that connects Pakistan to China.

They enjoyed exploring the spellbinding wonders of the majestic valleys, the grandeur of the lofty peaks and the breathtaking beauty of the meandering rivers.

We reached Kaghan, in northern Pakistan along the fast flowing, cold and clear waters of the gushing Kunhar River. This was a treacherous narrow one-way route on a high altitude.

We were there for three days, to inhale and absorb the natural splendour, with the genuine people of these remote highlands.

Our onward plans changed due to a blockade following an avalanche. It was very disheartening, as we were now, forced to return from Kaghan, instead of continuing with our plans. Our itinerary to travel this route was to view the rock carvings and inscriptions that are along the Karakorum. The carvings are like a travelogue and history, left by invaders, traders and pilgrims, who passed along the trade route, few dating back between 1000 and 5000 BC.

It is said some several years ago the Indian and Eurasian continental plates collided causing colossal pressure, while forcing the earth's crust to buckle and producing these towering mountains of the Karakorum.

We were left with no choice but to return; and more than a little disheartened, and decided to stop in Taxila; a centuries old city, in Pakistan's Punjab province. This was worth the detour, as history unfolds itself on arrival. Without wasting time, we decided to visit the museum and spend the whole day, fully absorbing the past civilization and its ancient relics.

I remember vaguely this visit to the Taxila Museum at a young age.

It preserves and presents the treasures of the Gandhara civilization, the cradle of Buddhism and display a vast collection of Buddhist sculpture and coins; from the first to the seventh century.

It is a little off any major route, but its location is there because most of the collection has been excavated from the nearby Taxila valley, the main centre of Gandhara. This city is a UNESCO world heritage site and was once, a noted center of learning. It was also to feature on the Silk route for several centuries. When this route became insignificant, the city had lost its importance and now only the ruins remain.

I was quite young when I visited, but I relived the visit, going down the memory lane, recalling all the lovely experiences, with my parents.

Though I myself do not remember the finer details of this visit, a photograph has captured this memory so well; I holding my parents hands, my right hand clasping my mother's hand, while my left hand tightly held my father's. However, the one admonishment that I still distinctly find resonating in me was, "Don't touch anything, this is a museum."

At that age, I hardly knew what a museum was! All I could see was old objects and statues, displayed inside glass cases. I was so scared of the thought; that they may also put my grandmother in a showcase.

I have a flash back of Buddhist monks engrossed in making a colourful palette of beautiful circular designs in symmetry. For sure, I was fascinated; still, not allowed to get close with the admonishment, "Do not touch". My father, knowing the young artist in me, had explained later, that what I was fascinated by, was a complex art of sand painting, embodying compassion, and that the monks would sprinkle millions of coloured sand grains, in different directions in a circle to create them. Painting with coloured sand is still a highly recognized form of Tibetan art. For them this is a universal symbol with an inner meaning which is meant to prompt the viewer to share the feeling and pain of others and motivate compassion for all humanity. They call this 'Mandala', which itself means 'Sacred circle', the essence to represent wholeness.

This artwork with different colours and patterns, which charmed and captivated me as a young child, denotes rich symbolism. It is believed that the yellow colour specifically evokes the message of compassion and in their culture, a way for spiritual development.

I was later surprised to find out how some societies have a way to inculcate empathy in them and sense emotions in others. This is a sensitive trait, which they develop through art as its medium, motivating compassion.

This fascination of mine with visual learning took me to some destinations, where their museums were repertoires of history, and which inspired me to chronicle it in my painting.

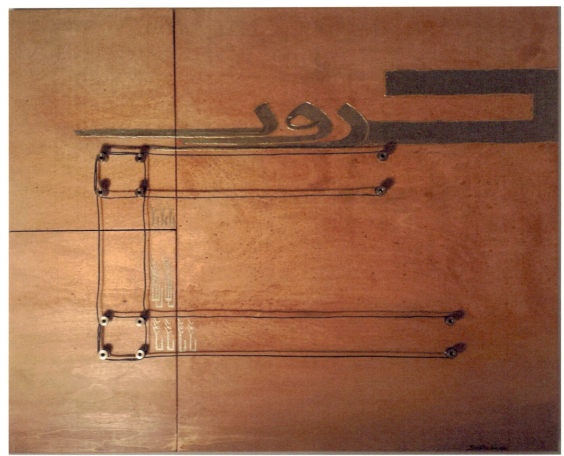

Sabiha Imran

**'Hudood' - Boundaries**

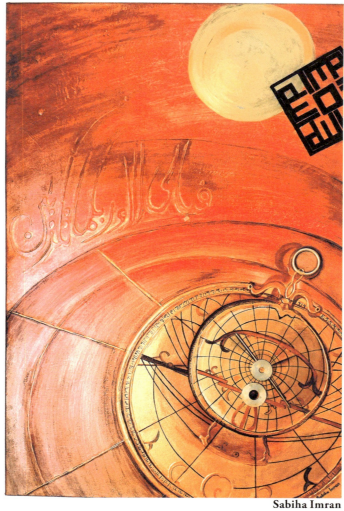

Sabiha Imran

**The Star Searcher of the Celestial Sphere**

**Journey Through The Shifting Sands of Time -**

Sabiha Imran

**History at a glance - From the Umayyad period in the 7th century, followed by the Abbasids, the Fatimids, Ayyubids, Mamluks, the Ottomans to the Mughals in the 16th centuty.**

These peeks into the past have been reflected in conveying my thoughts on canvass, as well as some mundane and ordinary things, that were visible as mere fleeting glimpses, during the journey.

As Saadi, a Persian poet of the medieval period has said,

> "A traveller without observation
> is like a bird without wings."

For me, this aspect was an uplifting experience and come to form the grounding for my art education.

It was a feeling of moving forward, yet going back at the same time.

Viewing the museum from Cairo, to the Topkapi, the Doha Museum, to the Louvre, the British Museum, to the Metropolitan and the Smithsonian; and still a few more - It was spellbinding, to say the least!

This time, the much awaited, treasure trove of Islamic Art was travelling towards us – to North America at the Aga Khan Museum. This was to bring to us the glorious reminders of the intellectual, cultural, artistic, and religious traditions of Muslim communities past and present serving as a cultural outreach towards the west. It houses the private collection of His Highness the Aga Khan, who is an avid collector himself; and enjoys the support of a generous contribution from his family. They seem to have a keen eye in recognizing these rarities. The museum's presence here was to give me a unique chance to be a part of its global humanitarian causes.

The serene environment of this museum certainly is a haven for the senses, along with its unique collection, but what struck me most, was the interplay of light and shadows created in some geometric architectural designs of this complex, which were ubiquitous.

The concept of light was a theme envisioned by the Aga Khan himself and he quoted in this regard the great Rumi:

> "The light that lights the eye, is also
> the light of the heart, but the light
> that lights the heart, is the light of God."

**"Ecstasy" - Sema ceremony; a miniature of Whirling
dervishes engraved on pewter**

I was prompted to engrave it on pewter for a 3 dimensional effect to reconnect and re-ignite the same energy that I felt, while attending the Sema ceremony. The Dervishes while whirling, have their arms open, embracing all humanity with love, expressing emotions and to achieve wisdom.

Truly he had ensured, that not only 'The light is ever present' but pervades throughout the building in many ways.

The 'Inner light' certainly is omnipresent.

I once got a chance while escorting the visitors inside the gallery to watch a photographer in the inner courtyard of the museum; deeply absorbed in his attempt to produce powerful irresistible images, in capturing the infinite qualities of light.

Seeing me watching so keenly, he was to eloquently remark to me, "It is a symphony for the visual senses."

I thought to myself, that my own passion to capturing light on canvas, and his passion for doing so through the lens were so similar. Witnessing him capture the images with such precision was truly uplifting! The Divine brilliant light has always fascinated our intellect with its aura of dazzling colours and amazing reflection.

I found this a perfect place, a deeply immersive experience for me, to be in an institution, so deeply respected and involved in humanitarian causes to volunteer, where the foundation's mandate, truly encompasses compassion, which is primarily just for the sake of God alone. Their service to humanity was something I respected, with its ethical perspective of inclusiveness of all faiths and respect for life; as they strive to promote a world, where all human differences are valued.

I recalled the intuitive term 'Ubuntu' that I had once heard, listening to President Obama's speech at Nelson Mandela's memorial.

As from a personal perspective, "Ubuntu" defines the essence of being human, which captures the same mandate as that which I experienced of the Aga Khan foundation. President Obama said, "Ubuntu is a word that captures Mandela's greatest gift: his recognition that we are all bond together in ways that are invisible to the eye; that there is a oneness to humanity, which we achieve by sharing ourselves with others, and caring for those around us".

# CULINARY OASIS

Toronto'15

This was an unusual transaction!

Immigrants all over are drawn to places where they can not only connect to people of their own ilk, but also to re-live the mouth watering exotic taste and aromas of their favourite food. One wonders if it is companionship or the palate that draws people to such watering holes.

The fondest memories that we are nostalgic about, is the taste of the delectable food. We keep reminiscing about the taste that lingers on with us, of our mothers home cooked meals, and our frequent enjoyable visits to restaurants where the food was almost addictive. Those culinary masterpieces, rather than the ambiance were the reason for visiting such otherwise mundane outlets.

One such place that we discovered by chance took us partly on a subcontinent's journey, a "Desi Dhaba," creating a contemporary fusion of where East seems to meet with the West. It became a favourite with us simply because of the homely feeling and appetizing food. However, what mattered at this casual street food eatery was the pleasant demeanour of the owners, who personally ran the whole show of welcoming, preparing and serving the mouth-watering delicacies with joy and their expectations and appetite filled beyond their wildest dreams. Visitors to this small and unpretentious out-of-the-way place, were seen and treated not as customers; but as devotees of this temple of flavours, and as honoured guests.

The young owner Jigar, always seemed genuinely pleased at seeing us. His whole personality showed his great zest for life.

He always came and served us himself, most often, he would sit with us and we would get into a very interesting conversation in this informal family lounge like atmosphere with oldies soundtrack, softly playing in the background.

Waving at us from the open kitchen, and even before we could order, he would prepare our favourite dish and gleefully bring it to our table. Leaving the table, he would say, "Your ginger tea too would be on its way," as he knew that was our inclination on every visit. However, he suggested strongly in a low tone, as he moved towards another customer's table,

"Try our popular yoghurt drinks, Ayran or Lassi. All our customers love it. You probably will love it too." Always torn between the salty and sweet, it was a difficult choice. Without a second thought, we quickly jumped at his suggestion of cold and delicious concoction.

As he was leaving to prepare the drinks, I happened to glimpse at the today's special on the menu and noticed that they were also offering 'Faluda.' The name certainly does not convey the sensuous drink that it really is. The description itself was so enticing for all customers. It is a concoction combining rose syrup, vermicelli, Basil seeds, and pieces of jelly with milk, often topped off with a scoop of ice cream. What a deadly cocktail, the fragrance of rose, the sweetness of the syrup, the cooling of the chilling. How could I ever have resisted it!

The availability of exotic drinks tempted us to go there often. On one of our visits, while parking are car, almost at the front of the restaurant, we noticed that there was a big "For Sale" sign displayed on a restaurant, adjacent to their place.

As it was very popular, at times this restaurant would be over crowded, inconveniencing the customers and even impeding the service. I casually used to tell him, "My dear brother, I think you need a bigger place now." He too would agree with us saying, "I too realize this."

A fortnight later, we visited this eatery again and saw the "Sold" sign on that same restaurant adjacent to them. We thought to ourselves; wish they were the ones who had bought this place. As with its thriving business, it was in dire need of its expansion. With that thought resonating in our mind, we went inside. Jigar, as soon as he saw us, came running to tell us that he had bought the next-door space! We were extremely happy for him, and wished him well, expressing the hope that he had struck a good deal.

The story that he told us in response amazed and delighted us even more, while at the same time reflecting on his personality and compassion.

He told us, "Though I could have negotiated a better price, I instantly decided and agreed to the price demanded by the owners." Continuing he added, "The owners are old and of retirement age, with not much to look forward to. So I realized whatever I paid them, would be their last big paycheck". "I on the other hand am still young and can work hard to gain greater success."

His reply made me think-- How great some people can be! This was a true reflection of man's innate goodness and bearers of such noble thoughts; thinking above self. Generally, business deals are transacted with the objective of making a profit, but here it was a transaction inclusive of a true good deed done so subtly. I expressed my great admiration for this young man's noble sentiment, and wished that his business would thrive and grow because of his humane gesture.

He seemed to live by his motto "Live to give and you will never run out of things to give."

His words, and this saying which I have shared with many, reminds constantly of thinking above self.

By Divine grace, this culinary oasis is now flourishing and providing succour and pleasure to many.

# BEYOND THEIR DREAM

Riyadh '82

And mine too!

With my son tightly holding my hand, I was waiting anxiously in the well-lit sanitized corridor of a hospital to meet the visiting Professor and Pediatrician, to get his second opinion about the recurring infection that my son had been experiencing.

At the central nursing desk, a family was also waiting ahead of me for information. Their desperation was justified; with one infant in the stroller, and the toddler in their arms, coughing and sneezing incessantly.

I was anxious, as I waited for my turn. Even stepping back from this infectious area, a foot and a half or so away, really did not matter much. With a slightly raised voice, I asked the nurse, how I could get in touch with the visiting paediatrician.

Without any eye contact on her part and with a blank expression, I was asked to wait. By now, my patience was running out, and I asked another nurse the same question, who replied confidently, "Dr Faez would soon be coming on his round accompanied by students." Certainly, they would befit from the wealth of practical experience of this highly acclaimed specialist, one who had the honour of having more degrees than a thermometer.

Standing quietly, I heard the footsteps of the approaching students, all clad in white gowns, but even then I could recognize the doctor, due to respect he was being shown and his very dignified bearing.

I interrupted, and hesitantly narrating my genuine short story, requested, if he could kindly give an appointment or a few minutes from his busy schedule, to see my son at his convenience. He too, asked me to wait in the adjacent waiting room.

This was comforting enough.

Few minutes later, he came with his students following him, and gently asked me to take a seat; and with his expert and thorough approach, asked my son's recurrent condition and symptoms. His demeanour and comforting tone was enough to put us at complete ease. After a thorough check-up, he suggested a few tests and told me he will then advise me with his assessment and diagnosis after seeing the results. Back then, the patients too received printed copies of these.

This hospital was a bit far from our home.

Two days later, I received a phone call from the doctor's office that the results were ready and if I could come and pick them up otherwise they can post it at our address. However seeing our address, Dr Faez very kindly offered to pass by your house, to save us from going all the way to the hospital to collect them". The accommodation provided to him by the hospital was not far from our home.

In the evening, he did pass by our house to drop the results as promised, assuring us that everything is fine but that it was necessary to have follow-up.

I could not believe his kind out of the way gesture.

The next evening, we visited him to thank him for this graciousness and his time.

We seldom got a chance to meet him and his family, as being a consultant; he travelled constantly and extensively dispensing his knowledge and a healing touch.

Little did we know then, that getting accidently acquainted with him and his family in such unusual circumstances would be the start of another very beautiful friendship.

"A journey is best measured in friends,
rather than miles."
Tim Cahill

California '09

After a very fulfilling career in various countries, Dr Faez and his family were thinking of finally settling down.

Often, circumstances and different priorities dictate many of our decisions, which actually affect our lives and just as importantly, where we end up living. Sometimes it is one's ambition, and so often personal obligations that drives us to settle and live in a certain place.

When the time came for this charming couple to desire to settle down, they chose to do so in San Francisco, a place that has many reasons to nestle there - a sprawling and captivating city on California's west coast, which fascinates most, with its Mediterranean climate and the warm summers.

This being a great natural scenic location; people often fall in love with this place. The Pacific Ocean surrounds this peninsula, whose sounds and waves bring true peace and relaxation for the mind and soul.

The intrinsic beauty and the panoramic view of the bay were attractive enough to settle along the coastline. This could even be a bonus for some, to be neighbours with the rich and famous. At night, it looks like a queen's necklace, studded in diamonds, sparkling and exquisite.

This angelic couple, so succumbed to the charms that they decided to relocate and build a home there.

I was keen to know about the dream house that they had been thinking about before moving to this charming city, which harbours a vibrant cultural scene for art enthusiasts and nature lovers. Alongside, is the lure and attraction of the Silicon Valley, with the dot.com world, that is enticing enough to the tech-savvy young urbanites. No wonder, it is sometimes, referred to as the Paris of America.

They wanted a home just big enough and in harmony with the surroundings as well as in tune with the location on a mountain, where the beauty of flora and fauna is preserved.

This unique piece of land they bought was primarily due to beauty of the scenic vista of the Pacific. However being on the cliff presented its own challenges, which were expected; but few became apparent, once the work on its construction would start.

Their next major step was to choose an architect, who would, transform their dreams into reality.

In quest of their dream house, they recruited a team of professionals. Together with their architect, they also considered hiring a legal team to adhere to certain state zoning laws that were applicable in the Bay area. As this would help them attain permits, to live peacefully alongside the wild life of their environment.

Listening to them, how I wished, we too; the human race, would tap into the universal reservoir of compassion, for living peacefully and amicably with our fellow human race.

The couple had been collecting clippings and taking pictures of some of the one-of-a- kind houses, built on a cliff, which at the same time, also gave them a chance to savour and enjoy those off route, small hiking adventures. With moments of some scary unexpected encounters with deer, coyotes, and the furry squirrels that casually passed by.

Moreover, Dr Faez had said, that as much as it was enjoyable and fun clicking the camera for ideas, their effort was to no avail, as each house highlighted a different facade, due to its unique location.

Once they found the architect of their choice, the planning and designing of their dream house started to take shape, that was spread over a few months. As much as the would-be homeowners, the builders and the architect too, began to look forward to this challenging project.

Upon completion of the drawings and plans, the work started on digging the foundations. The location was breathtaking, yet presented quite a few challenges by being on a hill. There was a slight climb to the site, as it was on a slope. Hence, the workers had to go up the naturally landscaped winding hill, lined symmetrically, with the hibiscus woody shrubs. The orange flowers of the California poppy, strikingly beautiful, appeared to be friendly enough with the Australian tree fern; all flourishing blissfully in this wilderness. This enthralling wide trail, being a bit secluded was very quiet.

I noticed that during our conversation, Dr Faez, did not somehow seem very enthusiastic about mentioning their dream house.

Nevertheless, while listening to them, I on my part got transported to this beautiful world, even before he had completed his tale of events.

This being on the rock, the workers had to dig with great meticulousness. Initially our friends and the workers did not notice anything unusual, as everyone had focussed on the drilling. After a while, they noticed that during the periods of lull when they stopped digging for a short time to rest, they could clearly hear the sounds of many animals, the denizens, and original inhabitants of these hills. They observed this on and off commotion, happening for a couple of days. As the weekend approached, they suspended the work to bring in supplies.

I noticed that there was a serious tone in their voice when sharing all this with me, and I too, was serious, in listening to them with intent.

What was very apparent to them was that each time there was complete silence when the work was stopped. After observing this continuously for a few weeks, it appeared as the animals were protesting at their peace being disturbed in their habitat.

Our friends on noticing the uproar were so concerned and sympathetic to the uprooting of the animals; that they actually decided to give up the project of their dream house in that location!

However, their tone did suggest they were heartbroken, yet an obvious feeling of contentment seemed to prevail on their faces. As they told us, "The decision for us was plain and simple; we didn't want to disturb the animals that lived there, as that was their rightful domain."

The Bay area is blessed with an abundance of unique animals, where mammals, birds, reptiles, amphibians, fish and insects, all live together in the natural habitat of theirs. Some, of course reside in secrecy, inside the rocks. Nevertheless, they too play a vital role, in enriching the environment.

Initially, I had felt sorry for them that they had to abandon the project, but later upon hearing the story,

I was to find myself greatly moved, that in today's' world, there are still people with such values and true humanity in their hearts.

In a world where there is scant value for human life, and we learn of thousands of people dying due to neglect and apathy; here was an example for all, to inculcate in themselves empathy for all living beings, not just humans.

To me, their deed was a testament to true human compassion, which bears the appearance of a fable, but in reality, was very true.

# THE FARMHOUSE

Toronto'03

The beauty around, was not just in the gardens, but more so in their hearts.

This place nestled beneath the enormous old chestnut and maple trees spreading their arms all around; some bowing in humility, and some confident of their stand-alone power. Beautiful exotic plants and beds of chrysanthemums and hybrid tea roses surrounded this grey, Tudor style 19th century house; like a heavenly fragrant bouquet, backing onto the calm and quiet waterfront.

It overlooked Lake Ontario, which the heron language so eloquently describes as the 'Lake of the shining waters'; reflecting bright sunshine to further enlivening the environment and brightening the mood of the occupants; who too were in total harmony with the surroundings; exuding charm, grace and a certain aura. The graceful ripples on the water seemed to hold their beauty throughout the day and shimmered in solitude, to contemplate at night. Wow! This I thought was a dream setting.

Amidst this natural ambiance, 'Appi,' as we respectfully called her; was sometimes seen all groomed to match nature's perfection, with a windblown hairdo. The dirt and the mud on her jeans and gloves were like a badge of honour,

The covered porch of the slanted timber roof was also set among beds of chrysanthemums. Appi would sit here in her spare moments, making stuffed bunnies and teddy bears.

Her fine hair covered her forehead, and the black bifocals rested almost on the tip of her nose. Seeing me, she brushed away wisps of her hair over her face with her aged fingers, and adjusted the bifocals in their designated position, with her infectious smile.

Sometimes I joined her to help her make them. I saw her dedication in her effort and her attention to meticulous detail, in making these for the children at the hospital; those young bundles of joy.

Being a doctor herself, and having been blessed with a gifted compassionate heart, she often realized the vulnerability of the parents, noticing their despair in spite of the best treatment that was being provided. She had thought that her simple gesture could still bring a joyful moment and a smile on innocent faces and a comfort to the parents.

As Appi had observed, parents avoid giving toys to their children that are in the waiting rooms or inside the clinic.

Who would not love visiting this couple, sharing in Appi's wisdom, love and zest for life. We enjoyed visiting them even more! Not to say, that it was anything less enjoyable when they visited us.

Generally, we dallied around until sunset to watch the orange orb setting in the tranquil lake, as a gentle refreshing breeze blew across this tastefully landscaped garden.

One would imagine that they would have liked to spend the rest of their lives in such an idyllic setting. However, they had much bigger and nobler plans in life, opting to go back to a country that needed them.

They had planned to settle in their country farmhouse, near the cosmopolitan and urbanized city of Pakistan, Islamabad, which lies at the foothill of the Margalla hills, with a majestic view of snow-clad mountains of the Karakoram Range. This 25 acres sprawling farm was well laid out and distinctly showed the time and love that had been spent to harness and nurture nature within its precincts.

Amidst rows of orange and apricot trees, laden with fruit clinging onto the branches, like yellow sapphires and ruby red grape bunches hanging from trellises as carnations and geraniums aspiring from below to capture the sweetness above, everything seemed to merge joyfully in symphony with fresh green vegetables that were happily growing a few feet close to mother earth.

The heavenly intermingling of fragrance and colour of the mesmerizing blooms attracted the birds and butterflies, who happily waltzed in the air, in tune with the summer breeze. The chicken too shared their company moving around with freedom, preying on tiny insects and happily clucking away, feasting on what nature had provided them. This was truly a happy place for all. However, the fragrance of their inner heart was much stronger.

The love for their farm, and their fondness for nature, was always a major reason for their frequent trips back home.

Avoiding the sultry summer, they once made a visit in late autumn, which was in the middle of a typical monsoon. That year the monsoon was unusually powerful, and caused a number of flash floods, the torrents gushing with unusual force, finding their way along the easiest courses and washing away anything and everything in their path.

What made it worse was that the pitiful small dwellings at the foothill of the mountain ranges with unstable slopes, had almost been washed away by the raging flood torrents, creating landslides, and some extent of damage occurred, with glacial-fed mountain streams.

The villagers had to flee to save themselves and their families. They had scant notice and not enough time to take their meagre belongings, and those that managed to salvage a few, felt themselves lucky.

Many of the mud houses had collapsed, and were washed away, while some still stood with leaking roof, while all bedding as such soaked in water, just cooking food also have been impossible, for their clay ovens were destroyed. What an ordeal!

Those dwellers, who had managed to save their wooden charpoys, clung to and perched on them, with sad tense grim faces, pondering on what the future held for them.

Realizing the vulnerability of these dwellers, on noticing the havoc in their area, the kind-hearted farm owners thought of providing shelter to their workers. They drove down to bring the young and the elderly to safety. The children hesitantly, yet excitedly jumped into the van, as most of them had never sat in a car before. Their innocent faces, happy and curious on sitting in the car, enjoying the ride, appearing unaware, that they had been rescued, and transported to a safer place.

The delight of these families at living in the farmhouse enjoying a warm bed, and a hot meal; as if enjoying room service in a hotel was indescribable.

In this caring environment, they temporarily forgot their hardship and the worries that had befallen them. I remember my generous friends telling me, how they had enjoyed the pleasant sight of an old couple, holding hands as they watched television into the late hours of the night at their place, an experience they never shared before.

This was to prove to be a paid vacation in a resort for their workers and their families. One can only guess their feelings.

Then, as Mother Nature stopped playing hide and seek with them, their lives slowly returned to the usual.

Having a soft corner for everyone, they thought of laying the groundwork for constructing simple dwellings for these families, as they had seen that they had experienced similar situations earlier. Starting on their plan, they soon realized that the area around the village had no electricity, nor the availability of easy water.

As the plight of these afflicted workers touched their hearts immensely, they took it upon themselves to find ways to alleviate their problems caused by the absence of these very basic needs.

In this regard, they considered the various options before them; digging of tube wells, the use of tankers to supply water on a regular basis, and even building of rain catchments to trap and store the rainwater.

Finally, they opted for digging a canal from the rivulet running behind their lands. This was a major project because of the hard and rocky terrain, and the lay of the land as well as the distance involved. The project proved to be more difficult than they had originally thought.

Coming up against many hurdles, some were natural and others manmade. Using all their resources, tact and diplomacy and a heavy dose of perseverance and commitment, they finally achieved their goal after a couple of months.

This, as anticipated was a thrilling day for all the dwellers seeing the canal reach the village and the water, gushing down. These anxious people, young and old had been gleefully watching, helping and participating over the past months, the digging of the canal towards their area, and just could not imagine the change it would bring in their lives. The women were particularly happy, as in the past, they had to go each day to where water was available to collect it, with heavy pitchers on their heads. Each moment was a new experience for them, even the sound of the generator.

The construction of the dwellings was next to follow under Appi and her very co-operative husband's supervision to ensure that the work was done satisfactorily without any wastage of money and time. On completion, the worker's families, all excited, happily bought their meagre belongings to start a better and easier life. On their settling down, Appi visited these families. The innate eastern culture drove them to take a house warming gift on their visit to their new dwellings. This is something, which perhaps is a norm in every affluent household, but to which, these poor people are not accustomed to.

As they stepped out of their car upon arrival, the children of the workers saw them carrying a big carton, ran to help them. With excitement, all huddled together in anticipation of seeing what was inside!

As soon as they saw them take out the television, the children started jumping in sheer delight. This was a big surprise for them. Overjoyed, the hard working people of this now small but developed village, started to look forward to the evenings, when after finishing their food, they could watch the news, the latest soap operas and pop singers. The starry nights spent with fellow dwellers, listening to the flute and relishing their hookahs, all in preparation for a good night sleep, would now be truly forgotten forever.

This wonderful display by our generous friends, and their unique sense of social responsibility was amazing. It seemed that they were taking care of this farm only to help the people of this small village. What a perfect amalgam of Mother Teresa and Florence Nightingale!

The small community of this village availed of the fresh produce from the farm every day. Appi used her considerable medical skills to look after their health needs; also taking it upon herself to teach the children. She religiously held classes at 9 o'clock at the farm. A strict disciplinarian with a commanding personality, she must have been quite firm in carrying on with that routine for all I know. I was overwhelmed to see her small van, converted into a mobile library, which she would drive to the village.

Seeing her, I wished I could join her in this small, but important mission. Their care and concern for others, was simply amazing.

For such a humble couple, this setting was a place that perfectly suited and matched their simple life style.

Like a stately, caring guardian, this farmhouse warmly held everyone in its arms.

"The meaning of life is to find
your gift. The purpose of life
is to give it away."

Pablo Picasso

# DESTINY

Her empathy found a solution, in spite of all the odds. - It shook me to the core as I listened to her....

There was loud clapping and a standing ovation from a packed crowd in Toronto's historic Massey Hall. It was a spellbinding experience and a treat for the mind and soul to attend this Massey lecture.

These lectures have established a place for themselves and have become a Canadian institution, as well as an annual highlight of the cultural life.

After this thought provoking lecture from the human rights scholar and lawyer Payam Akhawan, everyone had walked out having received a powerful message.

In brief, "Despair and cynicism is effortless. It does not take anything to say I am so depressed. The world is terrible. But get up and do something."

With this, thought for the day, we stepped out on the elegant street of the theatre district; with high-end restaurants on either side, teeming with people, lounging after enjoying the theatre experience; while on the same street, some homeless curled up in cold weather, trying to sleep on the sidewalk.

It is always difficult to see these two so disparate sights, side by side.

With these wandering thoughts in our minds, we were looking for a quieter spot among those upscale bistros, to have an enjoyable, yet meaningful conversation with Baji and our other friends, who were here on a business trip.

Walking around the corner, we were surprised to see a 'Chai shop'. This was a little unusual and certainly a new fad in the west.

After our long walk, we entered this restaurant and sat down to have tea. While we were preparing to order, a girl bought a tea caddy for our selection. Running my fingers through this array of herbal teas, I had to make a quick but difficult choice, as 'Deep green embrace', with its unforgettable aroma and flavour was available. My taste buds really enjoy that, but to give my friends company, I too decided to have lemon Green tea. As expected, it was lusciously evocative.

Sipping green tea reminded me of the words of Sen Soshitsu, an Urasenke tea master XIV of the Urasenke School of Japanese Tea Ceremony:

> "In my own hands I hold a bowl of tea, I see all of nature represented in its green colour. Closing my eyes, I find green mountain and pure water within my own heart. Silently sitting alone and drinking tea, I feel these become a part of me."

After having undergone the moving emotional experience, listening to this lecture, we continued our candid conversation, with the aid of another hot cup, this time of Kashmiri Chai. I was sipping this beverage after a very long time, the taste of which I had acquired earlier. This amazing pink beverage, made with the same leaves as green tea, is brewed in a special manner.

Baji's gestures, her eyes, all resonated beautifully with her inner true self. I just could not stop listening to her! Only surprised to know that she is someone who is full of the milk of human kindness,

I realized that the enlightened always find goodness wherever they settle, while the purest spread goodness and dispense kindness to whomever, whenever, and forever.

Many a times after spending a few years in a country, one starts to feel settled and well adjusted. However, most often, the chances of posting on a different assignment, after a period always looms over the horizon.

At times, a few fortunate ones have choices to lead their life in a country they love, maybe because they were born and raised there, and want to continue living as their ancestors and parents lived on that land. Then there are the enterprising and adventurous ones, who take bold steps to fulfill their dreams and strive to accomplish their goals in a strange land. Aha! If you even ask a gypsy, he too will come up with a fair reason of his nomadic meandering life.

The rationale of selecting an option, without a fixed menu, realistically depends on individual's set of circumstances.

Baji, as we lovingly called her, hailed from Peshawar, a city in the rugged northern tribal region of Pakistan. The inhabitants there, are known for their honest-to-goodness true nature and hospitality. The couple had moved because of their posting from Melbourne to Karachi where they settled down in an upcoming neighbourhood, where new phases of development were in progress those days.

While sharing with us, Baji sometimes seemed to be happy and contented, while at times sad, all her mixed emotions exhibiting at the same time, which I remember to this day.

Not too long after their settling down, and in their usual day's routine, Baji and her husband stepped out for a little stroll on a street outside their house to avail of Karachi's pleasant evening. It was a quiet, starry night; and both were engrossed in talking with each other. While the chowkidars, some whiling away their time smoking hookah, some in deep slumber on slack jute rope charpoys and guarding the under construction houses in their dreams. The honking of the cars and the barks of the dogs did not seem to disturb them. Rollicking Bollywood songs from their transistor radio were a great lullaby for these sentinels.

As they continued walking, they heard a child crying, but they hardly gave this a second thought, and almost ignored it, as it was nothing unusual. However, after a while, when the crying had continued unabated, it struck then, that the child could be unattended.

Worried, they stood still; silent; trying to determine precisely where the sound was coming from.

This area being a new development, only a few homes were completed, and some were still under construction; with vacant plots here and there among a lot of bushes.

The child was crying persistently and it appeared for sure, that there was no one around him.

Instantly, they came back inside their house, picked a torch, and asked their driver to accompany them. The chowkidars too bought along their kerosene lanterns to help locate and find the child, and they began to search for the spot in the bushes. This at night was not easy, amongst those thorny bushes.

Finally, they were able to find the crying baby nestled in the midst of dense wild bushes.

They picked the child and decided to bring him inside their home, wrapped him in a soft muslin cloth and went around the neighbouring houses to find the grieving parents in order to hand him over.

The little child seeing new faces all around him, was obviously scared, continued to cry, refusing even the water offered to pacify him.

Within a short while, the homeowners, the neighbours, all gathered to help locate the missing parents. Despite hectic and intensive search, they had to come back with the child, without being able to locate the parents.

It was already past midnight. Baji gave the child a bath to calm and soothe him. Oiled his tanned dry flaky skin and dressed him in clean clothes provided by a kind neighbour.

This little boys bright doe-eyed look, carried an expression of vulnerability, innocently gazing around, as everything was strange and alien to him.

Days then weeks and months passed, yet no one came to claim this little bundle of innocence.

Taking all precautions and everything into consideration, they decided to follow the call of their conscience and to take care of him and bring him up themselves.

With the tender, loving care that he was receiving, the child very soon developed a bond and started connecting with the ever so kind family.

The neighbours and friends on hearing the incident helped and contributed generously, which turned out to be a God sent baby shower.

A few months later, Baji noticed that the little child was unable to put pressure on one of his legs while walking. She decided to take him to the hospital for a clinical examination that provided affordable, quality healthcare.

The doctors were hopeful, if given proper care and treatment, he would be able to function well in a few years. Baji made the initial payment, and requested her spouse and friends to contribute to have enough funds for the child's ongoing treatment. The hospital too supported this genuine case, by charging a minimal fee. Finally, the treatment began.

Three years passed by in the blink of an eye. Their next posting was coming close. Baji began to get increasingly worried and perturbed, as she had taken a huge responsibility on her shoulders for the upbringing of this child.

At this stage, one of their friends, who had been witnessing their devotion to the child during this time, wholeheartedly came up with the offer to take this huge responsibility while they were away. The hospital and the doctors too were extremely cooperative in administering good medical care during this period.

Meanwhile, Baji too had kept in touch with her friends and the hospital, for the regular update of the child.

On their visit home sometime later, she was overwhelmed with joy to see this boy running towards her. With welcoming open arms, and holding him tight, tears of joy rolled through her eyes and contentment filled her heart, as she caressed this, young toddler. Both seemed to have developed inextricable bond with each other.

As much as it was satisfying for them to see the little one cheerful and healthy, it was also a challenging and tough decision time for them, and a lifetime commitment, as they wanted to relieve their friends from the responsibility, even if temporarily. The best solution that they felt under the circumstances was to send him to a boarding school, which they finally did.

It was very difficult for them to part from him, for it was like saying farewell to their own child. As by now, he was very much a part of their small, loving, and caring family. Hence, they made necessary formal arrangements, to furnish him with every necessity.

The child visited them every second year so that he would not miss them and the home environment, and they continued with the exalted commitment of theirs, alongside their other ones.

These were the only parents he would know, and theirs would be his home.

God had certainly made it a destiny for the innocent child to be raised at the hands of a compassionate, caring person; one who could easily comparable to a mother, who unselfishly and unconditionally raise and nurtures him.

After listening to her, I reflected that often charitable causes are planned; but in their case, Baji was put in a situation where she had to forcibly make instant decision to dedicate her life to supporting this child. This was an even bigger charity, all on the whim of hearing the cries of a baby.

This had changed two lives forever, one for the giver and equally for the receiver as well.

My mind was in two different zones; the first being Baji' story and the other, the message by the noted scholar; Payam Akhawan, "Empathy will always find a solution and apathy will always find an excuse." Baji's compassionate heart had found a solution.

"There are so many of us out there, each in our own way, trying to make the world a better place."

This always make me think that even the smallest act of charity can mean a lot to someone else.

# THE MAN - TOUGH YET SOFT

We were in a city that dominates the skyline, with modern architecture, surrounded by artificial lakes, and a vibrant life style that thrives through the sandy Arabian Desert, which leads into the Empty Quarter. Here desert hyacinths and acacia trees do not shy from emphasising their resilience. The Hajar Mountains rise on its western side with a natural water inlet, running north and south of the city, further beautifying the landscape.

Interestingly, Dubai is on the path of many migratory species, and a home to a colourful marine life; which serve as a magnet for just not the birds, but also for people from all over. Few for adventure, some for the opportunities and for many, maybe just to escape from their humdrum existence; thus over a period, it has resulted in offering so much to the now cosmopolitan population.

I felt that over the years, I met people who have left an impact that has always remained with me with the deepest respect for them. I was fortunate enough to have met a couple of extraordinary people; some with no money, but possessed a heart of gold and one or two with power, having reached the pinnacle of success, filled with a sense of patriotism.

One early spring, when visiting Dubai, we were fortunate to be invited for tea, along with another dear friend, to the home of a man who had faced some of the toughest challenges in life, faced bullets, having fought in two wars, served his country and reached the highest echelons - in both civil and the military. He is General Pervez Musharraf, ex chief of the Pakistan army and its former President.

This was a private invitation from a Statesman, and an occasion to remember. His home was modestly appointed; simple and elegant,; but the occupants were dignity personified, as well as articulate and authentic, one that rarely comes across these days.

Upon arrival we were escorted to the living room, where our host, Pakistan's previous President; General Pervez Musharraf, himself graciously welcomed us. I was immediately struck by his presence, a figure larger than life, who carried a certain aura around him that spoke for itself, and yet so humble and unpretentious.

Our exhilaration resulting from a most enjoyable conversation, was further to be enhanced by an excellent high tea; a case of 'Double Double'.

Our conversation was interrupted, when an attendant entered and respectfully informing the President that the food for Amma was ready in her room.

Excusing himself, he got up and went into an adjacent room. I could see him give a searching look at the tray, and then kissed his 92-year-old mother on her forehead, before proceeding to feed her with his own hands, spoonful by spoonful. I was able to see all this, while I admired the pictures of the president with the leaders of the world, on the wall.

I was simply overwhelmed to say the least by what I saw.

Seeing him so engaged, we then decided to take our leave, not wishing to intrude on this very private and precious moment. Sensing that we were leaving, he insisted that we stay a bit longer. However, we felt it prudent not to intrude and inconvenience him in any manner further. At this, he got up and accompanied us to the elevators; a gracious and moving gesture indeed.

Once outside, our friend mentioned another humane side of this Statesman which was to highlight further his kind, caring and magnanimous character, and the environment in which he was raised.

While driving back, our friend shared with us a very moving incident that she remembered from his childhood. Once, while playing in his home, he saw a furtive movement, and realized that there was an intruder in the house. He ran to his mother to let her know; and the mother shouted for help. The neighbours on hearing the shout quickly responded.

The intruder found himself surrounded and fearing punishment he begged for mercy, pleading that he was very poor and hungry and had not had anything to eat for a number of days. Hearing this, the mother in her kindness, had not only forgiven him, but had gone on to arrange to feed him.

This compassionate gesture was to affect the man so deeply that he later often used to visit the family, in order to pay his respects in expressions of gratitude.

People's compassion regardless of their status has never failed to amaze me; especially in the case of our visit to the President, and what we had seen with our own eyes, was truly delightful. Somebody of the status and position that of a President, a man carrying the huge responsibility on his shoulders of running a country, tending to his mother in such a caring and loving manner, that he chose to do everything for her himself.

Needless, to say his gesture had touched the core of my heart very deeply, and strengthened further my belief in the innate goodness of man.

**With General Pervez Musharraf,
Former President of Pakistan at his home**

# AN UNFORGETABLE TRIP

"Travelling - It leaves you speechless, then turns you into a storyteller."
Ibn Battuta

Ibn Battuta was one of the history's great traveller and scholar. In the 14th century, at the age of twenty-one, he left for Mecca and journeyed from N. Africa to China and back.

Jordan 2013

We understand, comprehend, and react differently to all that we see and in all that we do in our cycle and spectrum of life. Often, all this is so beautiful, that it is beyond our expectations and sometimes along such a different tangent that it is incomprehensible. These highs and lows are what make life so interesting.

I always look forward to a new morning, as each day brings boundless new challenges, opportunities, hopes, and creativity. Every dawn is the first day of the rest of our life.

Talking about the new and the unexpected, I found myself once, going on an unforgettable trip.

This was my second trip to Jordan. My first visit was in my lovely twenties as a newlywed. I was delighted simply because I was going to a new country, sightseeing, browsing in curio shops, and even picking up a local hand crafted magnet, made me happy then. Little things give me pleasure, even now.

With my innate curiosity, I enjoyed the historical sites; standing amongst them, with a big smile on my face, and besides the ancient columns, for a quick, yet memorable photograph. I must admit, I later had regrets that in those carefree days I had little or no interest in history.

The second visit was to be much different.

With our youngest son, Omar, we visited the ancient city of Amman again. This historic place has its own beauty, being built on seven hills, reminding me of the city of Rome, which too is referred to as a city of seven hills.

I contemplated on the number seven, and it struck me that it seemed to have so much significance in many different scenarios.

We have seven days in a week, seven beautiful colours in a rainbow, seven notes in music, not to mention the seven seas, the seven voyages of Sinbad, as well as seven continents. Then the Quran as well refers the presence of seven heavens, (Quran 7I.15); we also circumambulate the Kaaba and walk between the hills of Safa and Marwa in Mecca, seven times - This was certainly something to ponder.

Numbers are pervasive throughout our lives. Some numbers carry mystical and strong meanings - be it as a historical, geographical, or religious connotation.

The trip to Amman was nothing short of an incredible journey, filled with extraordinary happenings and encounters that surpassed my expectation and were well beyond my imagination.

**A glimpse of the amphitheater in Amman, Jordan**

**Temple of Hercules - Amman Citadel**

All I can say is: this was my unspoken desire, which was now being fulfilled.

Our Bedouin driver cum tour guide Bayan, was a godsend. He was a simple, friendly, energetic young man, a native of Wadi Musa, a village close to Petra. He seemed to know all about the historical hidden treasures that lay under the ground and below the skies.

The Nabateans had chosen Petra as their capital. Romans too had realized the importance of this strategic location. The trade caravans at the time frequented this route; known as the great Incense route.

This whole area is steeped in history.

Before heading on the King's highway, we wanted to have a quick stop over at the citadel, which interestingly is on one of the seven hills. This has been a home to many civilizations; the Roman, the Byzantium and the Umayyad, as is evidenced from the stone structures.

Making a short detour from this point, we managed to make a quick visit to the Greco- Roman city of Jerash, where ruins from the same periods still stand.

We were next heading towards Petra on the famous route, the King's Highway. As the name suggests, many kings travelled on this route, whose pathway beautifully follows the Great Rift Valley.

Tired after a long day, the fresh summer breeze for us was like a lullaby, putting us to sleep. Yet the breathtaking scenery was to prevent us from succumbing to its soothing caresses.

Just as I was about to doze off; the driver suddenly mentioned about the cave of the seven sleepers, (Number seven again) which is also near Amman in the village of Rajib. This suddenly piqued my interest and made me pay attention. This story, is described in the scriptures and delivers a powerful message.

The Creator put them all into a deep sleep for 309 years in the cave, to save them from the wrath of a Pagan king, who persecuted believers for their faith.

It was perceived as a miracle when they woke up three centuries later.

The story had always captivated me, as I myself often recite this beautiful Surah (Chapter), which bears the title of "The Cave."

On knowing that the cave where this miracle happened was nearby, I simply desired to visit this place. This distinctly created in me a sense of euphoria.

Bayan seemed to be spiritually inclined. While driving, he blissfully, started to recite verses from this Surah, which he had memorized with great devotion. Looking at him, one would have imagined he would be listening to some pop music, rather than so devoutly reciting.

Every moment amazed me after that and the charm of Petra and the joy of visiting it had diminished considerably.

Bayan also mentioned about the two castles further up the road. We thought of availing the opportunity of seeing them, before the sun went down as we had ample time at our disposal. However, the time was not enough, to see them in detail but barely sufficient, to have a glimpse of history.

We drove along, enjoying the raw beauty of the vast expanses, along the serpentine road, up to the Kerak castle. Believed to be the most well preserved in an area that was once a home to the Nabateans, the Romans, and the Byzantines.

However, the signs and remains, of these once mighty Powers, were merely visible to us as ruins.

Kerak castle had been built by the crusaders in the 12th century and served as a fortress between Jerusalem and Aqaba. Later it had fallen after a siege by the troops of the Muslim Sultan Salahuddin Ayyubi. He was the first ruler of Egypt and Syria and the founder of Ayyubid dynasty which had followed the previous three prominent dynasties to rule in this region, the Umayyads, Abbasids, and Fatimed Caliphates. The influence of the period of the Crusades, followed by that of the Arabs, was clearly visible in its architecture.

In order to see another fort, we took a short detour on this quiet unpaved road, and availed the opportunity to visit the Shobak Castle built by the crusader king Baldwin. This abandoned place was still and soundless, with nary a soul to be seen. I sensed the quietness as part of its appeal, but without serenity and tranquility.

Strangely, however, when we stepped out of the fort, the serenity in the surrounding open area was pleasing and noticeable. The breeze that moved freely was now playing hide and seek, as it meandered between the empty walls, and the columns, that were once standing tall, well guarded from even the sound that permeated this plateau. By now, the sun had started its slow descent, barely enough time to see their glorious past in detail.

This secluded fortress on a rocky mountain was built to protect the road between Egypt and Damascus. It was on the pilgrimage and caravan route. After many lulls generated by several truces, this too was to be seized by Salahuddin's troops; later to be occupied by the Mamluks. The view of this dramatic hill standing 1,300m above sea level is splendid, with fruit trees below.

It was twilight. We left as the horizon's brightness gradually faded, all now in preparation for a good night's rest.

I wished we had more time to absorb its charm, and observe its history unfold itself. Shobak had served as a strong hold for the Crusaders, then the army of Saladin and later by the Mamluks, who created the greatest Islamic empire and ruled Egypt and Syria between the 13th and the 16th centuries.

Continuing are journey after this detour of visiting these two forts, who were in hold of different dynasties; we were still 40 kilometers away from Wadi Musa 'Valley of Moses', the nearest town to Petra, driving past the rocky cliffs and scanty wooden hills. Our anticipation was running high in expectation to see the capital of the Nabateans, who were nomadic Arabs. It is known as "The Pink City," once the center of trade on the ancient world's spice and incense route, famous for its breathtakingly elaborate, natural carvings in sandstone.

**Treasury (Al Khazneh) sculpted from
the cliff centuries ago**

**Standing in awe at seeing the remains in the rock cut tombs
of the once powerful empire.**

We entered Petra through a narrow deep gorge, 'The Siq', flanked by high cliffs, a natural geographical feature created by a deep split in the rocks, which served as a conduit for water supply to the town of Wadi Musa. As the brilliant light meandered through all its crevices, we with a distinct sadness, saw the tombs of the Nabatean kingdom,

**The Siq**

As we crossed this pathway, I remembered about my childhood trip to Ziarat in Pakistan; once a British hill station to be etched in my mind to this day.

The spring water falls through the gorges: similar, though not so deep, narrow openings in the mountain rocks, creating the same colossal dramatic effect, amid the juniper forest. These 'Tangi's' meaning a tight space, were breathtakingly beautiful in their own way.

It was amazing to see the cascading colours of brown, beige, and mustard of the range, which gradually merged and continued until the Red sea.

**Sandstone rock in pink hues, in the rose city of Petra**

I was captivated and awe struck on seeing the grandeur, beauty and scale of this natural wonder; considered by many to be one of the Seven wonders along with Machu Picchu and the Great Wall of China - the number seven again popped up amazingly.

We drove a few kilometers along Jabal Haroun, 'Aaron's Mountain' and stopped for a while at a point where we could have a glimpse of his tomb, his final resting place. Aaron was the brother of Prophet Moses PBH; and a prophet himself.

Our intentions of climbing to it faded, as we noticed the steep climb. Still we felt half satisfied with the unobstructed view of the white dome that was visible. We stood at the foothill for a while, tears in our eyes, absorbing the aura of this place and the moment. We felt we were almost there and yet so far.

Filled with emotions at the sanctity of the site we had seen, we continued on our onward journey. Bayan suddenly stopped the car again and said, "I am going to give you another surprise." I was curious and eager to see the surprise that lay ahead, and quickly got out of the car to follow him.

Just a few steps off the road in a partly enclosed area, was a stream gushing out with sparkling clear water.

**The spot where Prophet Moses struck his staff and
the twelve springs gushed forth**

I began to wonder what could be so important about this place, with my mind unable to fathom the significance of this. Bayan too kept quiet, allowing me to continue my exercise for a minute, at seeing the water gracefully flowing in a direction unknown to me.

I too, looked at him with a blank impression, almost questioning him.

With a faint smile, he said, "This is the place where Prophet Moses had struck his staff on a rock and twelve streams had gushed forth, one for each of the twelve tribes.

There was silence, broken only by the soothing gurgling sound of the water, blissfully oozing out of the earth. I stood motionless; quiet for a few minutes, absorbing this. My eyes were looking at the clear water, while I sunk in deep thought, pondering at the historical significance of this spot, where the miracle had taken place.

Legend has it that the Nabateans had built the channels, which carried water to the city of Petra.

Visitors flocked to this area for centuries as it has so many significant sites along and off the road.

I wanted to stay a little longer, as these places always need time to absorb, but due to the time constraints, we had to leave and continue our journey on to Mount Nebo.

This route presented unforgettable view of the mountains in a blazing medley of colours; while at times they appeared to be in very distinct layers and sometimes the colours would merge, as if they were in love. That could only have happened by the Creator's will.

I could see majestic views for miles, contrasting with the desert scenery, the valleys, and the rest of the terrain. There was silence in these arid surrounding, though some shrubs grew here and there, like little green landmarks. Having lived in the Middle East, not to mention Pakistan for long periods and having travelled through the desert I could sense and see the similarity of this wilderness.

The serene and still Dead Sea, which is truly alive, despite its name, was now visible even from far.

Just a few kilometers later, we were travelling along the beautiful turquoise waters of the salt lake, some four hundred meters below sea level. This had once been a part of the Sea of Galilee. It was here that the clay jars with the Dead Sea scrolls, written in Hebrew, Greek, and Aramaic had been found.

Not being able to resist its beauty, we stepped out of the car, to inhale the fresh air, living the moment, enchanted by the view, of the very still Dead Sea. Every step along our path had been a bonus for us, with the faded colossal mountains in the background. The juxtaposition of water and mountains is as picturesque as it could be.

Next, we gradually drove the winding road of the thousand metre high mountain above the Jordan valley, which provided an even more spectacular view of the Dead Sea, allowing us to enjoy its serenity. Standing close to the water, and later, we had the opportunity to enjoy an aerial view of this deepest, hyper-saline lake in the world.

**At the Dead Sea**

**The path leading to Prophet Moses' memorial at Mount Nebo**

Tradition has it that it was from here that Prophet Moses could see the Promised Land. I felt blessed and privileged to be in a place where the Prophet of God had his exalted presence.

There was a feeling of calmness and serenity in this magnificent surrounding. How could it not be; as the Prophet Moses had left the aura of his presence there?

**The Memorial of Prophet Moses**

**Signpost on Mount Nebo**

**The valley below as seen from Mount Nebo**

It was truly a breathtaking vista of the sunset, to see the radiant orange ball gradually disappearing across the Dead Sea and over the gigantic hazy mountains and the beautiful valley beneath. The entire visit was captivating, with the feeling of being in harmony with nature. It is always difficult to express our deep emotions and to put those feelings into words, is never easy, unless they themselves flow of their own volition.

This had been for us a blissful day, with so many euphoric moments captured as we experienced firsthand - the sites of the history of the beginning of civilization. These cherished moments will always resonate in me with great feelings.

Famished by now, we stopped over to have a quick bite. This was a treat from Bayan, who by now was our good friend. And the good friend that he was, he just did not let us pay the bill. I kept thinking to myself, that in today's materialistic world, such simple, generous great people certainly do exist.

The thought of the day was clear to me that I certainly had not done anything out of the ordinary to get in touch with such wonderful people. It was my Creator connecting me to them; I will forever cherish that.

Considering the few hours still left to us, I felt unrushed, as I absorbed every minute of this environment. Even though I was physically tired, but emotionally and spiritually charged.

Being difficult to leave this place so early, we drove past Madaba, viewing the beautiful Byzantine mosaics on our way and were now approaching the village of Rajib near Amman, the site of the cave of the Seven Sleepers. Bayan pointed out towards the mosque, visible from far on a little hillock. The cave was adjacent to this hill, where few ruins dating back to Roman and Byzantine times still stood.

Bayan somehow managed to get the keys to the Cave's door from its guardian. I was, to say the least, more emotionally moved, than I can describe.

**Plaque of Cave of Kahaf**

**The Cave of the 'People of Kahaf'**

I could not believe that I was actually at a place that is described in the passage in the Quran - Chapter number 18 - with such a powerful and meaningful message.

Being there and somehow influenced by the surroundings, I was driven to further know, understand and appreciate the deeper meanings. It was an unbelievable and very enlightening journey.

Accompanying the guide, in great anticipation, we entered the cave in awe!

The door when opened created a strange unusual feeling. This place was big enough to accommodate ten people. The sleepers buried here; their graves, side by side, close to one another. On the sidewall was a sealed glass case, where their meagre belongings are well preserved. Faint light from a small opening on the roof lit up this space; which is now closed and protected by glass. The local authorities also placed the door at the entrance to the cave, in the not too distant past.

**With my son Omar, at the cave of the resting place of the Seven Sleepers**

**The graves of the Seven Sleepers, inside the cave**

It was just so quiet. I stood still, motionless, trying to absorb the unique aura that surrounds this place.

Difficult to fathom my presence there, I was truly floating in an ethereal world.

The journey to Petra and the unexpected trip to the Cave of the Seven Sleepers seemed like an unexpected gift in a series of my unpredictable exhilarating events.

As Martin Buber has rightly said,

"All journeys have secret destinations
of which the traveller is unaware."

My travels have truly expanded my horizon and have enriched my soul.

Every such experience has taught me that the people we meet in our lives have a profound meaning and influence in paving the path of our lives.

Had I been on the same trip in Amman, with another driver, who would have taken me straight to Petra and back to the airport, I would assuredly not have experienced the delight of visiting this mystical cave. Being with this particular person had provided me the chance to visit, a place, where my heart's deepest desires lie.

I have met many people in unusual circumstances in different countries. It were they who were to serve as a conduit in my spiritual journey. This encounter with Bayan, though apparently by chance, was preordained.

"I would like to live like a river flows, carried
by the surprise of its own unfolding."

John O'Donohue

# THE FRENCH CONNECTION

This was another one of our trips, which was to take me beyond the realm of seeing the beauty surrounding us, and to have an indescribable impact on me.

People travel far and wide, and the individual perspectives are what make things so different and interesting to each individual. It is in my travels that I have experienced rare, extraordinary moments in many ordinary and some unusual places. I am, reminded in this regard, of a few lines, from the Australian poet, E.J Brady's poem, 'Far and Wide'. Brady was the friend of the then Australian Prime Minister. He loved that country and the panorama of the ocean seems to have captured his young imagination beautifully in this instance.

He writes:

"Far and wide I have to wander, Far and
wide and to and fro

Let me see the sun-bars streaming, down
the valleys, ere the night; Fills the world
with pleasant dreaming, love and coolness
and delight."

This French trip allowed me to explore and witness, some unexpected wow moments.

Basking in the Mediterranean sunshine, we arrived at noon, in a region that gave us the opportunity to capture its essence, and drench into its history. This was a place that is in juxtaposition with the brilliant landscape along the mighty Atlantic and the undiluted beauty of the snow clad Alps, high in dignity, that look upwards directly at the vast, clear blue skies.

It so closely mirrored the Latin phrase "Veni, Vidi, Amavi"; (I came; I saw, I loved). The magical beauty of this place was to capture my heart.

On this trip, on a warm Sunday morning with bright sunshine, in the early summer of 1994 with a mild breeze blowing, it was like going through the splendour of the Renaissance period and a few centuries earlier. Just two-hour's drive from Paris, we ventured into the beautiful Loire valley, which was strategically important during the war years.

The quaint unspoilt villages of the countryside with the fragrant lavender and brilliant yellow colza fields everywhere, were creating magic along the river.

Many castles, dominated the area, like rubies and emeralds in a tiara. Some nestled in the thick green forests, with oak and hundred year old cedars, eavesdropping as they quietly stood to witness history and the life led by the nobles.

We saw a few on an island too, like some odd stranded swan afloat on the water, while a majestic stand on a terrace dominating the whole scene on a high platform to let the eye wander on the lush green landscape and the Loire River, meandering a few meters below.

In a small circle of daffodils, Magnolias and Azaleas, stood a stationary handcrafted weathervane like, signpost, pointing its hand towards the Chateau. This place certainly is the 'Pays d'Art et d'Histoire'- ('Land of Art and History').

Visiting these castles was like living in the medieval age. These chateaus seemed to welcome, but without the physical presence of a formal host. I strongly felt the desire to have a candid conversation, with the nobels, if only the walls could talk!

The heavy Italian influence pervading in them, greeted us with full force. The interiors had coiffured vault ceilings and elegant wood panelling, while its stone walls were adorned with renaissance tapestries and portraits, all hanging silently, echoing the absence of the kings and nobles who once lived there. A very distinct centuries old mustiness, discreetly reside among these thick empty walls. This gave a glimpse into the life of the Princes and the aristocracy though the centuries.

Their aesthetic passion for architecture was most visible in the impressive Chambord castle, the most recognizable in the world, with only 400 rooms.

Its emblem, 'Nec Pluribus Impar', Above all alone, against all, pretty much describes this castle. It had taken twenty-eight years to complete, but ironically, Frances1 lived there for only seven weeks (The number seven ever so strong again!) - leaving behind nevertheless a strong legacy in medieval history.

Enthusiasm builds up, as we continued along the valley, drenched in history.

According to historians, this region started acquiring its importance from as early as after its conquest by Julius Caesar.

During our four-day stay in this valley, we actually felt, we were living in the late medieval period, sensing the reality of the life lived by the Dukes and nobles.

Travelling on our planned route was almost like coursing through different periods in history; from the romantic 16th century renaissance to the era of World War II - all this encapsulated in just a few days.

We were enjoying the scenic landscape and the dreamy tranquility amidst quaint villages and through the countryside with surrounding verdant pastures and passing by the fragrant lavender fields and colourful fruit stands, laden with bushels of fruit and vegetables, which tempted us to stop for coffee. This small town appeared steeped in history and traditions.

Refreshed by the short break and resisting the fragrance of lavender trying to put us back to sleep; we continued our drive towards our destination. We were passing under the hide and seek shades of the age-old trees, that shimmered in summer's silent breeze.

After this pleasant drive, we reached the walled city of St. Malo. This 'cite fortife' now is different from what it was once, as most of it was destroyed during extensive bombing during the Second World War.

The walled area faces the English Channel, which is a narrow arm of the Atlantic Ocean, separating the southern coast of England from the northern coast of France in the Brittany region, inhabited by the Gauls in the first century.

We found ourselves wandering through history, along the walled city, which appears to sit beautifully with its emerald waters, its waves smashing against the natural terraces that are forcefully, battered by these. The seaport throughout the length of the coast was braving some fierce wet winds and high tides.

We could only enjoy this nature's spectacle only for a few minutes; as the sea swelled mightily, crashing dramatically to the walled city.

It was almost the end of summer, but the proximity to the sea, with the overcast sky and a strong wind blowing across the channel made us caress the northern winters again; forcing me with my numb fingers to tightly wrap the woolen stole around my shoulders. My hairstyle, if at all I had one, happily swaying with the swift dancing steps of the furious winds.

One cannot imagine from outside, the majesty of these gigantic stone walls, which appeared so comfortably to enclose this ancient city. The historic Romanesque-Gothic Cathedral, holding its presence in this old quarter, celebrates its presence as a pristine place of worship, with beautiful stained glass windows.

I managed to sneak in and take a quick peek inside the cathedral's interior, and admire what it beheld, as we walked and wandered around.

Interestingly, the French navigator, Jacques Cartier's grave is also inside this Cathedral.

He is credited, for not only with discovering Canada, but also naming it.

Cartier had sailed across the Lawrence River and opened to the French, the North American continent. He had actually lived in Saint Malo and travelled to my country, Canada, in mid 16th century from there.

A big thank you to Cartier, for discovering a truly wonderful land; which I now call home!

This visit was to touch me deeply and I really felt that I had made my French connection here in Saint Malo - I stood there feeling proud being a Canadian and its history.

While enjoying a little stroll, on these age old cobbled medieval streets, I felt they were certainly, not meant for women wearing heels. Though the stones now are flat and even, their worn out look, seem to make the place even more romantic.

Quaint looking shops and authentic French bistros lined these slow-paced old streets on both sides wherever we went.

While walking past these bistros, the aroma of freshly baked bread and pastries, tempted us, to find a nice spot, to relax and enjoy their delicacies, and the sumptuous taste of the French pastries.

As it was siesta time then, this less touristy area of Saint Malo was a little quieter.

Strolling past the enticing window display of a cafe, was so enticing that it propelled us to step inside without a second thought. The menu was so unique and interesting, I remember to this day. It was in the form of a poem with each verse referring to a culinary delight. As soon as my eyes landed on the word 'Chocolat', that was it! The Cappuccino and Chocolat St.Honore was simply mouth watering and luscious. It certainly was the perfect mid-day treat.

The unmistakeable presence of pink chrysanthemums in full bloom in the cafe certainly seemed to add to the pleasantness of its atmosphere.

In this small, well-tended garden porch, not far from our table sat a refined elderly man, in age-old tweed jacket and brilliantly polished oxford shoes.. While clearly displaying the inevitable, wrinkles of time, his accent, clearly suggested his British origin.

After we had finished our coffee, he very amiably invited us to join him, as he had noticed my curiosity.

His welcoming smile was wide enough for me to notice his missing teeth. With a sigh, he went down memory lane reminiscing, stating in a sad tone, "I came with my family and settled in Saint Malo when it was rebuilt after World War II."

Looking around, he said, "Saint Malo's walled city traces its origins from a Monastic settlement of the 6th century founded by St Aaron, who is believed to have spent his life here in seclusion meditating."

This man certainly knew his historical facts well, as we were to learn later, he was a graduate in history. In parting, the hallowed and wise person, after expressing his pleasure at meeting us, and noticing my passionate interests, strongly suggested that I should visit Mont. St. Michel and Lourdes, where I would feel a spiritual bond with the presence of an Ever-Present Supreme Universal Power.

We wanted to slow down with our itinerary, but the constraints of the pressure of time were to compel us to move on.

If one would consider the time from St. Malo to Mt. St Michel non-stop it would have been one and a half hour.

# NATURE AT ITS VERY BEST

I could not fathom this phenomenon, witnessing this spectacle was forcibly to strengthen my faith, further in the Ever Present Presence of the Supreme Power.

In great anticipation, we drove past some scenic trails to one of France's strategic, recognizable landmarks, and a seat of monastery, set in a mesmerizing bay. This is one of Europe's most unforgettable sights.

Mont Saint-Michel is a rocky island in Normandy, at the mouth of the Couesnon River forming an estuary.

**The Monastery of Mont St Michel, Normandy, France**

It is said that an Irish hermit had originally founded this place. This place has long inspired awe, and imagination.

The story of how the Mount, turned into a great place of Christian pilgrimage, is interestingly colorful.

I was captivated by this beautiful legend. In the 7th century, Archangel Michel appeared in a dream to the bishop of Avaranches and instructed him in strong terms to build a church, on this rocky tidal island.

Considered, as the foremost monastic establishment during the 8th century, it became a major destination for pilgrimage by the adherents of the Christian faith.

No wonder that this place, has been declared as a historical monument, and added to the UNESCO list of World Heritage sites.

My chance meeting with this random Englishman in Saint Malo Cafe was like enrolling myself on a crash course in French history. After that encounter we really found that we did not need a tour guide, nor Mr Google, as the elderly person had briefed us well in any case. Google also did not exist, back then.

In short, my curiosity to experience this place knew no bounds. This island clearly draws the eye from great distances as we travelled along the road towards the mount, we could clearly see from far, this "Marvel of the West". I could not contemplate its full magnificence, until it had gradually unveiled itself before our eyes.

The approach road was taking us straight onto the causeway, lined with Creperies and cafes. Difficult to resist temptation, we stopped at this charming place, with cosy ambience to have a fresh apple cider, and their signature pastry. This gave us a perfect boost of energy, for the climb we were to face next.

At that time of our arrival on the Mount, there was no water around the island, as it only surrounds it only at a certain time of the day.

We entered the fort through the main gate, which leads straight to the Grand Rue. The only way to the top and around Mt. St. Michel is on foot. The entrance, lined with souvenir shops was flooded with tourists. Browsing through this place, we went up the stairs to the forts rampart and took the quietest route up to the Abbey. It was a little tiring, because of the steep steps. We took short breaks in order to recover our breath, in the small gardens that are a delight throughout the various levels of the Mount. The climb was not easy, steep with sometimes spiral staircases, sheer drops, and uneven ground.

With gusty winds, reaching the top was quite an effort. For me it was cold. At times, I felt the winds would throw me off. The heavy people certainly appeared to have an advantage here.

Not surprisingly, there were railings in most areas. But this climb was worth it, as it boasts magnificent views of the entire bay. Nothing seemed to distract the peace and tranquility of this exceedingly stunning edifice, not even the high tides, and the fierce winds.

There is an abbey on top. The monks and nuns live on the Mount as a community. I learnt that they meet four times a day to pray and glorify God. Many pilgrims and visitors also joined them in this. On my part, I too found a quiet spot across this place to prostrate to my Creator on the cold floor, with biting wind around me, and the mighty ocean below.

Its Romanesque architecture was a significant feature. The lower levels have thick, robust walls to support the floors above and the towering upper levels.

With the excuse of recharging our energy, we decided to savor the culinary specialty of the Mount. We went straight to its famous restaurant, La Mere Poulard, world-famous for their omelettes since its establishment1888. A glimpse into their interesting wall of autographs from exclusive diners of over a century, made us travel back in time and history. 'Mere' was the title given to Anne Poulard, known in her day, for her talent, kindness, and natural generosity, preparing meals for the pilgrims.

Her recipe, have been a secret for 130 years. The expectation was as egg-spected, almost a live Martha Stewart show. Nothing extravagant, but certainly it was a extraordinary, culinary experience, as we watched them prepare the giant omelette few inches thick over an open fire, right in front of us.

Realistically an omelette is an omelette, one can add just about anything, to give it that fancy, personalized flavour and taste. This was an exceptional experience; more so of it being served at the top of the Mont, after a big climb.

Stepping out of this restaurant, I had a flashback of my mother, her face all sweaty preparing Sunday breakfast with our ever so favorite age-old omelette recipe of onion, tomato, and coriander with pan-fried Parathas. However, the special ingredient in that recipe was her unconditional love, which she would always lavishly pour into it. Such was its poignant taste that I savor it to this day. It was just so natural to connect that which we had just experienced to the past.

The view from the top was simply ethereal - a gigantic canvas of nature at its very best. Cascading shades of pure aquamarine, sapphire, shimmering deep and wondrous hue of royal blue, all seemed to dance in joy with the tides. The intermingling of this blue palette under one colossal, majestic sky was beyond description. I will never forget this afternoon, when the clouds moved gracefully amid the powder blue sky above me and the shimmering water with its meandering waves rising and repeating magically in this moment of my visual experience. This was a place where the sky and these waters meet mysteriously, without a line, break, or borders.

I began to think to myself, about how everywhere in nature, there are no borders; except where the land so beautifully meets the water, while protecting itself and all that is on it, sometimes boldly, while sometimes ever so seamlessly. However, where naturally land and sea, the skies and the earth meet so peacefully as dictated by nature; contrastingly human beings have created arbitrary and divisive artificial borders everywhere, be it to do with caste, creed, religion and country, dividing us in ways that were never meant for us to be divided.

The tides here, loud and furious were as high as 13 or 14 meters, these of course caused by the rise and fall of sea levels, which is the combined effect of gravitational forces exerted by the dominant participants, the Sun, the Moon, and rotation of the Earth. People claim that this tidal range is the highest in the world.

I still recall the scientific explanation for this, which I had learnt and recited like a parrot in 9th grade.

This made me understand, and witness it, like many other phenomenon on my journey.

After such a captivating and exhilarating day, we hurried back on the causeway before the expected time to witness the high tides that comes in very quickly, as it is said, "Like a galloping horse".

The time and the height of the tides are published daily. Bearing this in mind, we were just in time to be on land, across the island, as the bay until then, had still some water.

In great anticipation, when we arrived, many excited people were waiting to witness this visual extravaganza.

The clouds were in ecstacy, as if in a beauty competition, dancing with the waves of the ocean below.

It was mesmerizing to see those moving clouds above and their reflection in the water. Seeing was believing - truly magical!

It was early afternoon, when we were on the causeway, heading towards the Mont. At that time, there was no water surrounding the island.

Gradually, the unimaginable, colossal, gigantic waves started to advance and rise, inundating the entrance to the Mount, while forcing to slow down with bouncing frothy white foam. This dramatic scene took a centre stage for a brief one hour. There can be a difference of 50 feet between low and high tide - from no water around the Mount, to surrounding it, and then, forming into an island.

Soon the dazzling high tide, which had come with so much force, started to recede gradually, 15 km from the coast.

The fierce mighty Atlantic, stood there for a while, before it retreated out of sight, for me to live in that moment forever. I was truly in awe at this unforgettable spectacle, seeing the mighty Atlantic approach and recede. It was an amazing, rare phenomenon, to watch this natural panoramic show of these dramatic tides, that are a integral part of the mystique of Mont. St. Michel. As the sunset drew close, so was the end of the day. The vibrancy and brightness shifted from gold to silver, bringing serenity and quietness in its unlimited vastness, calling for deep introspection.

I was in praise of the Creator and His glorious and incomparable Supreme powers, as I stood on the edge of the causeway of this recognizable landmark, surrounded by the sound of the waves and limitless ever-changing view of the gigantic ocean, into the unknown and beyond its hidden mysteries that lay within, adding to the strength of my belief and faith. The literal translation for the Arabic phrase "Kun Fayakun"; "Be, and it is". When He decrees a thing, He only says to it, "Be", and "It is".

# MONUMENTO HISTORICO

The visit to Lourdes, a city that has its proximity to the Atlantic, was the continuation of my enriching journey, both spiritual and temporal.

This was a heavenly afternoon, with an overcast sky, slight chill and light showers,

We arrived in Lourdes, which is a small picturesque, beautiful town, located in the south of France in the foothills of Pyrenees Mountains with an elevation of 420 meters. During the medieval period, its castle has served as a protection from foreign invaders. The French captured this region from the English in the early fifteenth century. It was in early nineteenth century, by when Lourdes lost its military significance that its spiritual importance had started.

However, Lourdes was a strategically important, even at the dawn of the eighth century and the start of the Moorish invasion of the Iberian Peninsula in 711 A.D. launched first against Gibraltar under the banner of the Umayyad Caliphate from North Africa by the Arabs and the Moors who had converted to Islam.

The Muslims had possessed Lourdes for 46 years until the 7th century. The Pyrenees Mountains form a natural border between Spain and France. Tariq Ibn Ziyad, the Muslim commander, had initially led this campaign and crossed the Strait of Gibraltar from the North African coast. His success resulted in the capture of large areas of Spain.

Later, differences rose between the leader of the Moors and the King of France. The leader of the Moors surrendered, converted, and according to the legend, he was given the new name, 'Lorus'. The town he held was later known as Lourdes.

Reminiscing about the past as we strolled through the remnants of Moorish history, which still stood as a proud testament to its culture, I instantly thought of the grand Alhambra palace and fortress in Granada, and the magnificent mountains of Sierra Nevada, whose grandeur we were fortunate to witness. Both during the day, and then to enjoy its stunning view later by sunset, from a mountain across the fortress, for which we had to scale the medieval winding streets, paved with cobbled stone all the way to the Mirador de San Nicholas.

**View of the Alhambra from Mirador de San Nicholas**

Those moments also take me back to the lively square in Albayzin quarter of Granada, which has a 16th century old church, built on the site of the mosque, like many other in Granada. Few metres across is the first mosque, built some five hundred years later, where I had a chance to offer my prayers.

I remember sitting later in its courtyard, viewing the castle and reflecting on the many simple pleasures enjoyed during that trip, sipping Zumo de Naranja with simple Tostada con Tomate. This does sound exotic! These names in their original language do give them a more unusual flavour. But these were simply fresh orange juice, and a toasted roll with grated tomato, sprinkled with olive oil. Anything fresh is always tasty, especially when you are somewhat hungry.

While enjoying myself in the present, and contemplating the past, I was immersed in Moorish history, as I travelled back and forth in time. Centuries gone by, battles won and battles lost; power struggles continued to conquer, win, and control the vast empires.

In hindsight, power struggles, conquests and the control of vast empires, seemed merely to highlight the transient nature in the real sense. This was very strongly brought to me, while visiting Lourdes, It had also made me recall the indelible mark left by the Moors in Spain's myriad imposing landmarks, such as Alhambra, the Great Mosque of Cordoba, and the magnificent Medina Al Zahra to name a few, alongside the medieval castles of Europe.

**Inside Mezquita De Cordoba, Spain**

I kept thinking about my earlier impressions, formed during my visit to these places some years back. Then, I was more in awe of their grandeur and amazing architecture. Now, on this second visit twenty years later; my reflection on the fact, that these imposing magical monuments, though holding deep historical significance in so many ways, were now uninhabited, void of life and energy. One can only imagine their glory and grandeur during the time when their Dynasties were at the epitome of their importance and were lived-in and enriched by people, who imaginably contributed to the development of the arts, science, and culture. .

The history of the Moors was going through my mind as I entered the city center of Lourdes.

We were looking forward to see the fort first, as its majestic presence in the town could not be ignored.

This solid, stone-fortified castle strategically positioned on a high altitude, is thought to be the oldest such fortress in Europe.

To climb up to the fort, one had to be physically fit in order to scale these heights. We gradually climbed up the steep incline, and up to the fort, which without ignoring overlooks the town below.

This was a stunningly scenic place, where nature and history intertwine. The Pyrenees Mountains appeared to be a silent witness to this region's rich history with so many hidden secrets and tales to tell.

Below, we could see a train with its, loud and rumbling sound, winding its way to the next destination. The ride must be amazingly delightful as the track lay on a high ground along the undulating Gave River. The ducks float sideways along the fast flowing swift currents, and riding them, paddles back and enjoy another round. It was a real visual treat and a joy to watch this natural, live merry-go-round.

The lofty mountains, rugged in appearance and yet ever so compassionate, gracefully surround the city and gives way to the fast flowing river, Gave de Pau, which borders on land by a rock called Massabielle. On this rock near the riverbank is a natural, irregular shaped shallow Grotto or cave, in which the famous apparition of 1858 had taken place.

This place was very peaceful and serene, a slight breeze brushing my face; I stopped, and stood there for a while, enjoying the feeling and nature's beauty.

Tourists had filled the town holding umbrellas, in order to protect themselves from the slight drizzle and enjoying the sights, as was I .

Now and then, the sun would peek through the low clouds, further bringing its magic and energy to this place. The pilgrims, young and old, could easily be differentiated by their attire and demeanour. Yet, they appeared full of piety and steeped in the aura of the place.

The city of Lourdes is famous as a sanctuary and it is said, in 1858, a young catholic girl, Bernadette Soubirous was in the woods to collect firewood, when an incredibly beautiful girl, which according to Believers, was the Virgin Mary, appeared before her on 18 different occasions at Massabielle grotto. She was to tell the girl to dig the ground in a certain area. When the girl obeyed, a small spring gushed forth. Its water, has since been known to have healing properties.

In the vicinity of this sanctuary, I could relate to the feelings and emotions of the pilgrims at Lourdes, as I too had been on pilgrimage to Mecca, and places, which are sacred, or of special significance to me, where I had felt the same indescribable emotions, and a connection to the Creator and Supreme Being.

Seeing them drinking water at the Grotto, with total reverence, devotion, and faith, I compared it to my experiences at the well of Zam Zam in Mecca, where I too had experienced the same feelings and a gamut of emotions.

The spring of Zam Zam, has been continuously gushing water in a barren dessert since the times of Prophet Abraham (PBUH), and consumed by millions of pilgrims.

It has been an everlasting miracle and a divine gift to the devout since.

The similarities between the two diverse places, and the incidents associated with their origins, struck me forcefully; the miraculous appearance of water, and the reverence in the followers of the relevant faiths.

My travels have always served to impress upon me to recognize and acknowledge the many beautiful souls that are around us, and how common beauty is, if only, we take the time to do so.

Benjamin Disraeli, Former British Prime Minister describes beautifully,

"Like all great travellers, I have seen
more than I remember, and remember
more than I have seen."

On my return from Lourdes, I realized that wherever one goes in the world; though the physical beauty of each place may be different but the inner beauty within the people around the world is the same. We all have a connection with our Creator and we all connect differently, each one in his own way.

# THE AWAKENING

Whenever some close friends or relative came back after performing the pilgrimage, we always invited them to our place. I remember sitting with them and raptly listening to the narration of their physical and spiritual journey and the changes that it triggered in them.

One of their consistent message was their obvious transformation; and I inevitably found that the feelings that resonated in them with their narration would also echo in me; bringing tears to my eyes.

I was in awe of them, as they had been present in the holy city with hundreds of thousands of other pilgrims, renewing their pledge to God.

When I would meet them later, I could not fail to notice the change in them- most importantly, the contentment in their hearts. They were different but better people.

I observed them, overwhelmed with emotion and gratitude, and a sense of fulfilment that they had actually been present in the house of God. This raised the urge in me to also experience what they had experienced.

I probably had this latent in my inner being.

From a very early age, I had opportunities to visit the holy sites and always looked forward with great devotion to going there and be part of the congregation, leaving the pleasures of the world and all pretensions behind. Even thinking of this by itself made me feel contented and connected.

While the joy of performing the rituals and prayers was present, I still felt a void in me, as my spiritual connection was missing.

In all honesty; at that point of my life, I did not even know what spirituality was. That void in me made me want to understand the self-awareness that God has instilled in all of humanity, and which often gets neglected in our more worldly struggles.

It was my deep desire to visit again; and this time; not only experience the physical proximity to the house of God, but experience that spiritual connection that had been missing.

After a couple of years, I visited Makkah again and was thankful to God for again giving me this repeated opportunity and then a chance for me to be in a place where I felt the presence of pure thoughts, and to connect and comprehend, what I so much desired.

This time I was a different person, someone who had the choice and fortune to raise her children, and gone through the joys and tribulations of life, and has matured as a person, as a parent, and as an artist, and blessed to meet so many wonderful insightful people in my life, who were like my mentors.

They had taught me the wisdom in conducting my life in a more gratifying manner. I learnt not just to put focus on the rituals that I perform so diligently, but most importantly to feel and make the connection with the Divine.

Deep emotions rose in my heart as I was entering the awe-inspiring sanctum. I was desperate to have a glimpse of the Kaaba again; the resplendent black cubical structure draped by the Kiswa, embellished with gold Quranic inscription. It is magnificent in every way imaginable - just so powerful, that it took my breath away. No words can ever describe the true feeling of this experience; it can only be felt.

This was such a mesmerizing moment that I had even forgotten to pray; and found myself revelling in the presence and its majesty. I was there before dawn, the time when the orange ball of fiery light, the sun starts to peek from above the horizon; providing an ideal backdrop to the ever majestic Kaaba.

**My painting - 'Radiance'**

The sunlight that touches the Kaaba is in a way a reflection of the light that the Kaaba spreads over the entire world.

Devotees, all in bare feet, keep coming in and going out, from the different gates; in order to find a spot on this blessed ground, to bow their heads in prostration, denoting total submission to the Creator. Some have a rosary in their hands, their eyes glued on the Kaaba. The young and the old, tired after travelling here from all the corners of the globe, would nevertheless be seen totally immersed in their prayers despite their exhaustion. Some were so tired and weary that they would be lying down on the hallowed ground and resting with their eyes closed.

When the call for prayers resonated in the air like a clarion call it motivated all to stand up, creating a ripple and wave effect. Tens of thousands people stood up in rows, shoulder to shoulder in order to pray in unison, prostrating after each single call together. The amazing feature of this holy place is even if there is a congregation of tens of thousands of people, everyone gets a spot to prostrate and pray. It is just so uplifting and awe inspiring to notice the discipline and strength of everyone's faith together.

All would be focussed and engrossed in their thoughts and prayers, some with tears rolling down their faces, some serene ones reflecting the calmness and harmony in their hearts; alone in meditation, unaware of the hundreds of thousands around them. Some were still circumambulating in ultimate ecstasy. It was just so captivating.

This place is alive all the time, every single moment of the day, a place where the Prophets, their Companions, the Saints, and the Mystics circumambulated. The energy that I felt is indescribable. Each soul seemingly connected and immersed in meditation; as I too was trying to do.

Looking at the Kaaba, I was trying to connect to my inner self - the soul connection that we have with God. This was not only about the circumambulation around the Kaaba, but also my conscious attempt, to erase my meaningless negative thoughts and to have a clean heart.

The tears in my eyes were but a small manifestation of the overwhelming spiritual emotions. It was surreal; something that cannot be described. This place somehow made me reconnect back to my upbringing and life experiences, as religion and spirituality were always taught to me with great love, but seeing the Kaaba in front of me, brought everything together and made an impact on me in a way I cannot describe. This certainly seemed to be the beginning of understanding the wisdom and message behind the obligatory prayers and rituals. Making me conscious to love and serve humanity, inculcating a giving caring nature; and correct my own self rather than judging others. I was thanking the Most Merciful for guiding me to see within myself and realizing what it means to be closer to God.

I was very fortunate, that over the years, I was associated with some incredible people; ones who had great empathy and compassion for others and had dedicated themselves to alleviate the sufferings of fellow human beings, and had whole-heartedly immersed themselves in the noble cause. In hindsight, these kindred souls, had inculcated and strengthened in me the love for humanity.

Finishing my prayers, I supplicated for all the people who had helped me in my journey towards this self-realization; and thanked the Almighty Lord because the ultimate guidance is only from Him.

This emotion of true love can only manifest itself with the Divine presence.

I had been here many times before, but this visit encompassed a unique experience.

As a Swiss philosopher said,

'In the heart and consciousness of each Individual, there exists an essential and profound intuitive awareness and recognition of the presence of the "Transcendent". The human being has within it an almost instinctive longing for a dimension that is "Beyond".

T. Ramadan

Sabiha Imran

**Introspection**

Sabiha Imran

### Soul Connection

**It is only when one looks within oneself that the brightness of
the soul shines through. Every human being has a soul connection
to God. Unsurprisingly, the Arabic letter 'Alif' is the first letter
of the word 'Allah'.**

My life experiences and not just my religious teachings had aroused a spiritual awakening, and an awareness, which had brought me this much closer to God and His teachings. These were not just limited to certain rituals, but to a way of life. It taught me how to live my life in a balanced manner, and how to connect spiritually to my Lord, to whom we will all return.

Saadi, the famous philosopher, Sufi and a poet has expressed this so beautifully:

"You have no need to go anywhere,
Journey into yourself,
Enter a mine of Rubies
And bathe in the splendour
of your own light."

There was contentment and a magical beauty in departing from this blessed place. But my heart was still there, and I did not want to leave, wishing that time would stand still for me.

I left with these pure thoughts, and the realization that I should consciously connect to the Divine every moment at all times and not just in the holy sanctum, but everywhere.

My last few minutes, in the sanctum, were the reinforcement of this realization.

# THE JOURNEY GOES ON...

A prominent 19<sup>th</sup> century Persian and Urdu poet, Ghalib, eloquently expresses in a couplet:

> "When topics and subjects come in one's
> thoughts, then the sound made by the pen,
> resonates like the sound of angels."

In my life, events and reflections have indeed been like inspired flashes. These anecdotes and moments mentioned have not merely moved and touched me, but made me understand better, the rhythm of life.

This also reminds me of the Latin proverb, *'Verba volant, scripta manent',* that I came across in a community library.

It suggests, "Spoken words fly away, written words remain."

I started to write down my thoughts as I used to wield the brush in order to transport and express my ideas on the canvas. Creativity is expressed through various disciplines, but I can certainly say for myself that it has been easier for me to transfer ideas on canvas than to encapsulate them in the written word.

"Writing is the painting of the voice."
Voltaire

I came across a beautiful word in Arabic on my second visit to Cairo in 2012, which gave me food for thought.

This place had been again on my bucket list for a long time.

Cairo, Egypt's capital, is set on the banks of Nile River, known as a city of a thousand minarets, and houses not only the Pyramids, but also the second oldest institution of higher learning, Al-Azhar, founded during the 10th century by the Fatimid dynasty, which was to establish one of the greatest civilizations that encompassed the flourishing of culture and knowledge in all fields.

**At the Al-Azhar University in Cairo**

Driving through some of Cairo's narrow, winding, busy and chaotic alleys, we were looking for a parking spot. Though nothing in sight and still anxiously waiting, we noticed a car slowly reverse from a tight parking spot. Happy to notice this, but also a little reluctant, we somehow still managed to squeeze in, almost in front of a bookshop. Slowly, and taking a deep breath we managed to get out of the car.

A poster in bold Arabic text drew my attention rather forcefully. The poster emblazoned with the word "Al Tawafuq". With almost no knowledge of Arabic and my limited knowledge of Urdu, this word to me seemed derived from the word, 'Ittefaq' meaning by chance.

My curiosity drove me inside the bookshop. This was a perfect place for a book lover. I started browsing and hoping to pick up a nice coffee table book on Egypt. One could spend hours inside this quiet space and have a peek into some fresh thoughts, sensing the obvious indescribable musty smell of the old books.

At the payment counter, my curiosity made me ask the meaning of the word 'Al Tawafuq'. He explained it very well and in detail that it meant, - 'Coincidence'.

Sufis believe that there is no such thing as coincidence, and - everything is for a reason. They believe that, "Anything that happens, was actually meant to be", and my journey made me believe in this.

It was interesting for me to get to know the meaning of this word in this manner, in the fountainhead of this centuries old center of learning and wisdom.

This truly made me nostalgic and induced me to reminisce about the past and reflect on the people who came in my life; from my noble parents, family, and friends to the few I got to know by true serendipity. Some people come to create memories and leave, but those cherished moments are preserved while we hold on to a few who stay on for life.

The word 'Tawafuq' itself was true to its meaning: it is simply unbelievable that it caught my attention in this manner and then kept reverberating in me.

In life, I have come across so many new words in different languages; but this particular word ever so forcefully resonated in me, like no other. Sometimes, the reason for such occurrences becomes apparent only later. Hence, one of the reasons for this trip clearly appeared to have been the reinforcement of the meaning of the word "Tawafuq"; and a more lucid discovery, by me of the explanation of its significance.

Hence the title for this book - "Tawafuq".

It is my belief that there is no such thing as coincidence, but it is meant to be.

**'Tawafuq' ------ My thoughts on Canvas**

The few extraordinary and remarkable people I met, and came into my life were not a coincidence but 'Meant to be' and for a reason. They had an amazing effect on me with their love and wisdom, giving me a refreshing perspective to life that no formal education could have given. They were like pearls; one more iridescent than the other, developing gradually over a period, with brilliant lustre, unique in their own way, very rare. No wonder, pearls have come to be a metaphor for rarity.

These experiences and extensive travel to amazing destinations, has broadened my horizon and sharpened my perception and a penchant for reflection, as I witnessed the fusion of the splendour of human civilization and its accomplishments, alongside the grandeur and captivating natural raw beauty and wonders of nature that envelop the earth.

> "Once you have travelled, the voyage never ends; but is
> played out over and over again in the quietest chambers,
> that the mind can never break off from the journey."
> Pat Conroy
> American author

What struck me forcefully was that all of these were in some way or the other, manifestations of one single conjoined thread; of an entity, that permeates the whole universe, with its love, beauty, compassion, and power.

All the brilliant and astounding treasures that surround us, sometimes unknowingly, start creating a different perspective to life. As being the same individual, I feel I am more spiritually inclined and more receptive to the beautiful things that happen to us; with a very pragmatic view in spite of my constant struggle between reason and the spiritual side.

Aptly coined, this French phrase *'Joie de vivre'*- is a delightful way to simple living, reveling in every single moment, as happiness comes in many forms, and we should joyfully savour them all, appreciating, and relishing in the delights of even the smallest of pleasures. While recognizing our part in leading a passionate, meaningful life, with a compassionate heart; and the reason for the human existence to be seen, through a global lens.

"There is nothing more artistic than loving people."
Vincent van Gogh

Life is a journey; of challenges, and transformation; and mine were braided together and woven intricately with radiantly-coloured threads of learning from off-beaten paths.

I find that the following couplet by the famous humanist, Sufi poet Rumi very well captures the aspects of the journey.

"Your task"?
"To work with all the passion of your being to acquire the inner light."